THE RESURRECTIONIST'S DAUGHTER

VICTORIA ARDEN

PROLOGUE

The silence was as loud as any explosion, and just as perilous as any powder keg to the three figures hunched in the darkness of the graveyard.

THE COLD BIT into their bones, but they knew that in a few minutes, they would be sweating as heavily as dray horses hauling coal through the city's cobbled streets.

THE LEADER TOOK a slow measured glance around the churchyard and then pointed to a fresh pile of earth. His two accomplices stepped forward, shovels tucked under their arms.

"A CHILD?" one whispered, his voice caught between revulsion and relief that the dig would require less labour than a full-sized grave.

THE LEADER simply nodded and pulled his hat further down over his ears. He took a step back as the shovels, especially sharpened to make light work of the lightly frozen ground, bit into the sod.

THESE MEN WERE PRACTISED in their grisly craft. They ought to be, considering the dozens of graves they had violated over the preceding two years. In scarcely ten minutes, the burlier of the two struck something unyielding. His spade rang against metal like a church bell announcing the dead.

"QUIET," the leader hissed as his pulse started to race. He held up his hand as he scanned the graveyard, half-expecting men to emerge from the hedgerows and seize him.

"MERELY THE BRASS nameplate upon the lid," the larger man whispered, kneeling to brush soil from the small coffin with a leather gloved hand.

THE LEADER NODDED and allowed his heart to return to its slow steady rhythm. None of this ever got any easier. He knew they could be caught at any moment. He didn't know which he feared more - the authorities, with a probably sentence of death in front of a baying crowd, or the mob, who would string him up from the very oak tree he now stood beneath. He had witnessed what remained of resurrection men caught by an angry crowd: bodies left hanging from gibbet trees, eyes plucked out, tongues torn from their mouths as warnings to others in their unholy profession.

GIVEN THE CHOICE, he would take his chances with the magistrates. He would pled for this life - transportation to Van Diemen's Land seemed merciful compared to such butchery.

"LET'S GET IT DONE," the leader said, turning and jumping down into the grave alongside his men.

THE SMALLER OF the two pulled out a crowbar, and after a series of sharp cracks, the coffin lid groaned open. A sickly, sweet odour of decay rose into the air. They were just in time. After tonight, even the price for a child's body would drop considerably.

THE LARGER MAN pulled back the burial shroud covering the child's face. For the briefest of moments, the moon emerged from the clouds and shone on the girl's features. The leader took a step back. she bore an uncanny resemblance to his own daughter, safe in her bed at home. He gathered himself quickly. This was just a business transaction. He reminded himself of that and pulled a large sack from beneath his coat. The larger man made effortless work of lifting the child from the coffin and stuffing the lifeless body inside.

. . .

THE MEN CLIMBED out of the grave, and the leader resumed his watch, alert for any sound or movement, ready at any moment to give the order to flee. Yet nothing stirred in that unholy hour save barn owls and the restless spirits of the dead.

THE MEN REFILLED the grave as quickly as they had dug it. This was the most delicate part of the process. It had to look untouched. They could not afford to have this particular churchyard placed under watch. The only guarantee of future harvests lay in leaving no trace of their nocturnal labours.

THE LEADER CAST his eye over the freshly filled grave and nodded his approval. He took the shovels from the others, and the larger man hoisted their grim cargo over his shoulder as though it weighed nothing.

THEY DISSOLVED into the darkness like morning mist.

. . .

In less than half an hour, they would reach the teaching hospital. They would meet their contact, and another transaction would be complete.

That was how the leader tried to think of it. It was a business transaction. He was dealing in a commodity, nothing more. A commodity that would never run out. Death was certain in London.

It was an enterprise that promised prosperity for a lifetime.

The leader knew that for such a lifetime to endure, eternal vigilance was the price.

And he was fully prepared to pay it.

CHAPTER 1

The creak of the garden gate roused Elizabeth from sleep. Dawn light barely filtered through her bedroom curtains as she slipped from beneath warm blankets and padded across the cold floor to peer through the window. Below in the courtyard, her father hunched beneath the weight of a canvas sack slung over his shoulder, his boots caked with mud that left dark prints across the flagstones. His fine coat was splattered with something Elizabeth couldn't identify in the half-light, and his face bore the grey pallor of exhaustion.

Elizabeth pressed her small hands against the glass. Father never came home this late, or rather, this early. The household clock had only just struck five. She watched as he glanced furtively toward the street before hurrying across the yard to the garden shed, disappearing inside for several minutes. When he emerged, the sack was gone. He straightened his dishevelled collar, ran a hand through his tousled hair, and looked up at the house.

His gaze caught Elizabeth's. For a moment, surprise registered on his face, quickly replaced by a warm smile. He blew her a kiss and made a playful shooing motion, urging her back to bed.

Elizabeth waved, comforted by the familiar gesture, though questions bubbled within her eight-year-old mind. She returned to bed, but sleep eluded her as she listened to the quiet sounds of her father entering the house, the muffled splash of water from the washroom, and finally, the soft click of her parents' bedroom door.

"More tea, William?" Mary Flanders asked, her elegant hands poised over the silver teapot. The morning sun streamed through the dining room windows, catching on the fine China and polished silverware that adorned the breakfast table.

"Thank you, my dear." William Flanders looked nothing like the mud-splattered figure Elizabeth had witnessed hours earlier. Freshly shaved and dressed in a crisp business suit, he sat at the head of the table reading The Times, the very picture of Victorian respectability.

Elizabeth watched her father over the rim of her milk cup. How could he appear so rested after returning home at dawn? His eyes showed no trace of the exhaustion she'd glimpsed earlier.

"Elizabeth, you've hardly touched your porridge," her mother observed, her voice carrying the gentle reproach of a woman who had never known true hunger. At twenty-eight, Mary Flanders maintained the beauty and poise that had first attracted William's attention. Her morning dress of pale blue muslin rustled softly as she adjusted her posture. "We must leave promptly for the charitable ladies' meeting at ten. Mrs. Pemberton has specifically requested our attendance to discuss the winter clothing drive for the workhouse children."

Elizabeth dutifully took a spoonful of porridge. "I saw Father coming home this morning," she said, the words tumbling out before she could consider them. "Very early, before the sun was properly up."

The teacup in Mary's hand paused halfway to her lips. Her eyes flickered toward William, a silent communication passing between them.

William laughed, folding his newspaper with deliberate care. "What an imagination you have, my sweet girl. I've been abed all night, dreaming of ledgers and shipments." He tapped the side of his nose conspiratorially. "Though I did rise early to review some business papers in my study. Perhaps you glimpsed me taking a turn in the garden to clear my head?"

"But your boots were all muddy, and you were carrying a heavy sack to the shed," Elizabeth persisted, her brow furrowing. "I watched you from my window."

Mary set down her teacup with a sharp clink. "Elizabeth, it's impolite to contradict your father. And peering through windows at dawn instead of sleeping, what would your governess say about such behaviour?"

"Now, now," William interjected, his voice jovial though his eyes remained watchful. "No harm done. Children often confuse dreams with reality, don't they? I'm sure Elizabeth thought she saw something." He turned to his daughter with a wink. "Though next time you think you see a ghost or goblin, perhaps call for your mother rather than watching alone in the dark."

Elizabeth opened her mouth to protest but closed it again at her mother's warning glance. The porridge turned to paste on her tongue. She hadn't been dreaming. Had she?

"Speaking of business," William continued smoothly, "would you like to accompany me to the office today, Elizabeth? You've been asking to see the new shipment of Indian silks."

Elizabeth's spirits lifted immediately. "Oh yes, please!"

Mary frowned. "The docks are hardly an appropriate place for a young lady."

"Nonsense," William countered. "She'll remain in the office proper, not the warehouse floor. Besides, how else will she learn to appreciate the comforts our business provides if she never sees its workings?" He smiled at Elizabeth. "Every proper merchant's daughter should understand trade, even if she never conducts it herself."

Elizabeth beamed, momentarily forgetting her confusion about the morning's events. Visits to Father's office were rare treats, full of exotic scents and fascinating people. Perhaps there she might find answers to the questions forming in her mind.

The dockside office of Flanders Imports stood three streets back from the Thames, close enough to oversee shipments but far enough to avoid the worst of the river's stench. Elizabeth clutched her father's hand as they navigated the busy streets, dodging carts and street vendors hawking everything from meat pies to bootlaces.

"Mind your skirts, Elizabeth," William cautioned as they sidestepped a puddle of questionable origin. "Your mother would have my hide if you returned home soiled."

The office itself was modest but respectable, a narrow building with "Flanders Imports: Fine Textiles and Spices" painted in gold lettering across the window. Inside, two clerks hunched over ledgers, their quills scratching industriously as William entered. They stood immediately, offering respectful nods.

"Good morning, Mr. Flanders."

"Morning, Perkins, Whitby. This is my daughter, Elizabeth. She's come to inspect our operation today." William's voice carried the easy authority of a man accustomed to command.

"How do you do, Miss Flanders," the younger clerk said with a small bow that made Elizabeth giggle.

William led her through to the small warehouse at the rear, where crates of merchandise waited for distribution. The air hung heavy with the scents of cardamom, cinnamon, and exotic fabrics. Elizabeth inhaled deeply, closing her eyes to better appreciate the heady mixture.

"Here," William said, opening a small sandalwood box. "The finest silks from Bombay. Feel how light they are; like holding a cloud."

Elizabeth ran her fingers over the shimmering fabric, marvelling at its softness. "It's beautiful, Father."

As William showed her around, Elizabeth's sharp eyes noticed details that didn't quite align with her father's narrative. The warehouse seemed oddly empty for a thriving import business. Only a handful of crates bore recent shipping marks, while others gathered dust in corners. The ledger on Perkins' desk showed modest transactions: a bolt of silk here, a sack of spices there; nothing that would support their comfortable townhouse and her mother's fine dresses.

While examining a display of tea samples, Elizabeth overheard her father speaking in hushed tones to a well-dressed gentleman who had entered through the side door. Their conversation drifted across the room in fragments.

"...fresh supplies required by Friday..."

"...the educational institution has increased its offer..."

"...medical research demands the highest quality..."

The gentleman passed William a heavy purse that disappeared immediately into his coat pocket. No receipt was written, no entry made in the visible ledgers. The transaction complete, the visitor departed with a tip of his hat, never once acknowledging Elizabeth's presence.

"Who was that man, Father?" she asked as William rejoined her.

"Just a business associate, my dear. Nothing of interest to little girls." His smile didn't quite reach his eyes. "Now, shall we see if Mrs. Perkins has packed those biscuits I requested? I believe she's included some ginger ones. Your favourite."

Elizabeth accepted the diversion but filed away her observations alongside the mystery of the early morning sack and muddy boots. Something didn't add up in her father's respectable merchant facade, and despite her youth, she was beginning to recognise the shape of secrets in her household.

* * *

Elizabeth sat on the upstairs landing, her nightgown pulled around her knees and her face pressed between the wooden balusters. Below, her father welcomed visitors unlike any who called during daylight hours. These men wore rough woollen jackets and cloth caps, their hands calloused and their speech coarse. They spoke in hushed voices, but the night air carried their words up the stairwell to Elizabeth's straining ears.

"St. Bartholomew's is paying double for fresh specimens," one man said, counting coins into his palm. "More than worth the risk, I say."

"The Whitechapel cemetery has new burials in the east section," another reported. "Three yesterday, including a young woman. Good condition, according to the gravedigger."

William's voice was lower than the others, forcing Elizabeth to lean dangerously far between the balusters. "We'll need the wagon tonight. Harrison, you'll bring the tools. Morris, secure the route. We must be away before the moon rises."

Elizabeth's heart thumped painfully in her chest. Specimens? Burials? What business could her father possibly have in a cemetery after dark?

A floorboard creaked beneath her weight, and the men below fell silent. Elizabeth held her breath, pressing herself against the wall. After a moment, the conversation resumed, but with greater caution.

She didn't hear the approach of soft slippers on carpet until her mother's hand closed firmly around her upper arm.

"Elizabeth Anne Flanders," Mary hissed, pulling her daughter away from the stairs. "What do you think you're doing out of bed at this hour?"

Elizabeth winced at her mother's grip. "I heard voices. Who are those men? Why are they talking about cemeteries?"

Mary's face paled in the dim light of the corridor. For a moment, fear flickered in her eyes. Not anger at her daughter's disobedience, but genuine fear. Then her expression hardened.

"Your father conducts business at all hours. It's not for you to question or eavesdrop upon." She marched Elizabeth back to her bedroom, her fingers digging into the child's arm. "You will go to sleep immediately and forget what you've heard. Do you understand?"

"But, Mother—"

"Do you understand?" Mary repeated, her voice sharp with an emotion Elizabeth couldn't name.

"Yes, Mother." Elizabeth climbed into bed, but as Mary closed the door, she caught a glimpse of her mother's hands shaking as she clutched her dressing gown tight around her throat.

Elizabeth waited until the house fell silent before slipping from bed again. This time, she went to her window, watching the courtyard below. Shortly after midnight, her father emerged with two of the rough men, all carrying shovels. A small cart waited in the alley beyond their garden gate. Elizabeth watched until they disappeared into the fog-shrouded street, heading in the direction of the old parish cemetery.

She returned to bed, but sleep eluded her. Questions chased themselves through her mind until dawn painted the sky the colour of weak tea. Only then did exhaustion claim her, and she fell into troubled dreams of open graves and mysterious sacks.

The next morning, Elizabeth watched her father at breakfast. Dark circles shadowed his eyes, and he moved with the careful deliberation of a man nursing sore muscles. Yet he smiled and joked as always, complimenting her mother on a new bracelet that glinted gold and sapphire at her wrist.

"It's beautiful," Elizabeth said, studying the expensive piece. "Is it new, Mother?"

Mary's hand jerked slightly, sloshing tea onto the tablecloth. "Yes, dear. Your father gave it to me yesterday."

"A small token of appreciation," William

explained, patting his wife's hand. "A business success gift for my devoted wife who tolerates my long hours."

Mary's smile seemed fixed, her eyes never quite meeting William's. "Your father works very hard to provide for us, Elizabeth. We must always be grateful."

Elizabeth nodded dutifully, but her eyes remained on the bracelet. Had it really been purchased with money from Indian silks and cardamom? Or was it bought with whatever had been in that heavy purse passed in secret at the office?

After breakfast, while her parents were occupied with visitors, Elizabeth slipped into the garden. The summer air hung heavy with the scent of roses, but another odour drew her toward the shed where she'd seen her father store the mysterious sack.

The shed door creaked as she pushed it open. Sunlight streamed through dusty windows, illuminating ordinary garden tools hanging neatly on the walls. A spade, a rake, pruning shears, all perfectly innocent. The floor was swept clean, with no sign of the sack she'd seen her father carry.

Elizabeth stepped inside, inhaling deeply. Beneath

the expected smells of earth and old wood lurked something else: a sweet, sickly odour that made her stomach turn. She'd never smelled anything quite like it before, but some primal instinct warned her it was wrong, the smell of something that should be buried, not stored in a garden shed.

"Elizabeth? What are you doing in here?"

She whirled around to find her father standing in the doorway, his large frame blocking the exit. How had he approached so quietly?

"I... I was looking for the trowel," she stammered. "To dig up some worms for fishing."

William studied her face, his expression unreadable. Then he stepped inside, closing the door behind him. The shed suddenly felt much smaller.

"You're a curious child," he said, his voice gentle but serious. "Always watching, always listening. Your mother says you take after me that way. Your governess, Miss Willsey, has informed us how you are by far the most intelligent child she has ever had the pleasure of instructing. Well advanced for your years, she said, and that one day you will prove yourself and go on to do great things." He crouched down to her level, placing his hands on her shoulders. His touch was tender, but she couldn't step away. "But some things, Elizabeth, are too complicated for little girls to understand."

"Like what you do at night?" The words escaped before she could stop them. "With the shovels and the cart?"

Something flickered in her father's eyes: surprise, perhaps, or concern at how much she had observed. Then he smiled, the familiar warm smile that always made her feel safe.

"My work involves many aspects, some more... unusual than others. But everything I do is for our family's happiness and security." His hands squeezed her shoulders gently. "Can you trust me on that, my sweet girl? Can you trust that your father knows what's best?"

Elizabeth looked into his eyes, searching for reassurance. She loved her father, trusted him completely. Yet the sickly smell lingered in her nostrils, and the memory of those rough men discussing cemeteries echoed in her mind.

"Yes, Father," she said finally, because it was what he wanted to hear.

William's smile broadened. He kissed her forehead and stood up. "That's my good girl. Now run along and help your mother with her correspondence. She mentioned needing your neat handwriting for some charitable society letters."

Elizabeth nodded and slipped past him into the sunlight. As she crossed the garden toward the house, she glanced back to see her father still watching her from the shed doorway, his expression thoughtful. She raised her hand in a small wave, which he returned before disappearing inside the shed once more.

Something had changed between them. Some invisible boundary had been drawn. Elizabeth didn't understand exactly what her father did in the darkness, what filled those mysterious sacks, or why her mother's hands shook when she thought no one was looking. But she understood that these were secrets she wasn't meant to uncover, questions she wasn't meant to ask.

For now, she would pretend not to see, not to hear, not to wonder. But in her heart, Elizabeth knew she had glimpsed the edge of a shadow world that existed alongside their respectable life, a world her father inhabited when he thought no one was watching. And despite her promise, despite her love for him, she couldn't unknow what she had begun to suspect.

Some truths, once glimpsed, could never be unseen.

CHAPTER 2

Elizabeth's fingers traced the edge of the wooden panel behind her father's desk. Something wasn't quite right about it. While helping William organise his papers, she'd knocked against the wall and heard a hollow sound that didn't match the solid oak panelling elsewhere in the study. Now, with her father momentarily called away to speak with a visitor, her curiosity overcame her caution.

At ten years old, Elizabeth had grown more observant, more suspicious. Two years of watching her father's nocturnal activities had taught her to notice small inconsistencies, like this panel that didn't sit flush with its neighbour's.

She pressed gently along the edges until she felt a slight give near the bottom corner. The panel swung inward on hidden hinges, revealing a shallow compartment carved into the wall. Inside lay a stack of leather-bound ledgers, different from the business accounts that sat openly on her father's desk.

Elizabeth glanced toward the door. Her father's voice still rumbled from the hallway, deep in conversation. She pulled out the topmost ledger and opened it, her heart quickening as she recognised her father's neat handwriting.

The entries were methodical, arranged by date:

March 15, 1847 – Guy's Hospital – Two specimens (male, 40-50 yrs; female, 20-30 yrs) – £15

March 22, 1847 – Royal College of Surgeons – One specimen (male, 30-40 yrs, exceptional musculature) – £12

April 3, 1847 – St. Bartholomew's – Three specimens (two male, one female, all fresh) – £20

Elizabeth's mouth went dry as understanding dawned. "Specimens" weren't exotic imports from India. The payments came not from textile merchants but from medical schools. The sums were far larger than anything recorded in the legitimate business ledgers, enough to explain the fine furnishings of their home, her mother's jewellery, and the comfortable life they led.

She flipped through more pages, finding detailed

records spanning years. Some entries included notes about condition, cause of death, or special requirements from the buyers. The most recent entry was dated only three days prior.

The sound of footsteps approaching the study sent a jolt of panic through her. Elizabeth hastily returned the ledger to its place and pushed the panel closed, scrambling back to her original task just as her father re-entered the room.

"Sorry for the interruption, my dear." William smiled, straightening his cravat. "Now, where were we with those shipping invoices?"

Elizabeth stared at him, seeing not the respectable merchant but the man who sold dead bodies to doctors. Her hands shook as she gathered the papers on the desk.

"Are you well, Elizabeth? You look rather pale."

"Just a little tired, Father," she lied, unable to meet his eyes.

Later that night, Elizabeth lay awake, the terrible knowledge burning inside her. The specimens. The cemeteries. The sickly smell in the garden shed. All the pieces fit together now in a picture too horrible to contemplate yet impossible to ignore.

The ledger felt heavy in Elizabeth's hands as she stood in the doorway of her father's study that evening. William looked up from his desk, his smile fading as he recognised what she held.

"Where did you get that?" His voice was unnaturally calm.

"Behind the panel." Elizabeth's heart hammered against her ribs, but she forced herself to step forward. "I found it this afternoon."

William's face drained of colour. He rose slowly from his chair, crossing to the door and closing it firmly behind her.

"Give it to me." He held out his hand.

Elizabeth didn't move. "What are 'specimens,' Father?"

A muscle twitched in William's jaw. For a long moment, he simply stared at her, calculation visible behind his eyes. Then he sighed, shoulders slumping as if a great weight had settled upon them.

"Sit down, Elizabeth."

She perched on the edge of a leather chair, still clutching the incriminating book. William poured himself a generous measure of brandy from a crystal decanter, drank it in one swallow, then sat heavily in the chair opposite her.

"You're too clever for your own good," he said finally. "Always have been. Just like me." He rubbed his hand across his face. "What do you think specimens are?"

"Bodies," Elizabeth whispered. "Dead people."

William nodded slowly. "Yes."

"You dig them up from graves and sell them to doctors."

Another nod.

"That's why you go out at night with shovels. That's what was in the sack I saw you carrying." Her voice rose slightly. "That's what I smelled in the shed."

"Keep your voice down," William hissed, glancing toward the door. Then, more gently: "Yes. That's what I do."

The confirmation hit Elizabeth like a physical blow, though she'd already known the truth. Tears welled in her eyes. "It's wrong. It's stealing. It's—"

"It's necessary," William interrupted, leaning forward intently. "Do you know how doctors learn to heal the sick? How surgeons learn to cut out disease? They need to understand the human body. They need to practise."

"But—"

"The law only allows them a handful of executed criminals each year. Not nearly enough. Without men like me, doctors would be cutting into the living without knowing what they're doing." His voice grew passionate, rehearsed. "Every body I provide saves dozens of living patients. It's not pretty work, Elizabeth, but it serves a greater purpose."

Elizabeth stared at her father, trying to reconcile the man she loved with this stranger who spoke so calmly of violating graves.

"The dead are beyond caring," William continued. "They're rotting in the ground, serving no purpose. I give them one last chance to be useful." He reached for her hand. "Think of all the lives saved by the doctors who learn from these specimens. Isn't that worth something?"

His logic sounded reasonable, yet Elizabeth couldn't shake the horror of it. "Does Mother know?"

William's expression hardened. "Your mother knows what she needs to know."

"But it's against the law."

"Yes." William's tone grew sharper. "And if I'm caught, I'll be transported to Australia for life. Our home will be forfeit. Your mother will be destitute. And you—" he paused for effect. "You'll be sent to the workhouse."

Elizabeth had heard enough stories about workhouses to feel a chill at the threat. Children separated from parents, meagre food, endless labour, disease, and death.

"No one must ever know, Elizabeth." William took the ledger from her unresisting hands. "Not your friends, not your teachers, not even your mother—though I suspect she's guessed much of it."

He crossed to a small table where her mother's Bible lay. The family Bible, passed down through generations of Mary's family, its leather cover worn smooth by years of devotional reading.

"Come here."

Elizabeth approached reluctantly.

"Place your hand on the Bible."

She did as instructed, her small hand dwarfed by the ancient book.

William placed his hand over hers, pressing it firmly against the cover. "Swear on your mother's Bible that you will never reveal what you know about my business to anyone. Swear it, Elizabeth."

"I swear," she whispered, tears spilling down her cheeks.

"Swear that you will take this secret to your grave."

"I swear."

"Good girl." William released her hand and

returned the ledger to its hiding place. When he turned back to her, his manner had changed entirely, becoming once again the affectionate father she knew. "I've always said you're special, Elizabeth. Clever enough to understand things beyond your years."

He reached into his pocket and withdrew a small velvet box. "I was saving this for your birthday next month, but perhaps now is a better time."

Inside lay a silver locket on a delicate chain. Far finer than any jewellery Elizabeth had owned before.

"Beautiful, isn't it?" William fastened it around her neck. "A token of trust between us. Our special secret."

The metal felt cold against Elizabeth's skin. She understood what had happened; she had been transformed from an innocent child to unwilling accomplice, bound by oath and bribe to protect her father's crimes.

"Now," William said brightly, as if they'd just finished discussing a school lesson, "I believe Cook mentioned apple tart for dessert tonight. Your favourite."

Elizabeth nodded numbly and left the study, the weight of her father's secret hanging around her neck like the silver locket that had sealed their pact.

* * *

THE CEMETERY GATES creaked as mourners filed out after the burial service. Elizabeth stood beside her mother, watching the grieving family of Mr. Jonathan Perkins accept condolences from the assembled crowd. Her black mourning dress itched in the summer heat, but she maintained the solemn expression expected of a child at a funeral.

Since discovering her father's true business two months ago, Elizabeth had begun noticing things she'd previously overlooked. Like the young woman currently approaching the widow with an expression of perfect sympathy.

"Such a terrible loss, Mrs. Perkins. Mr. Perkins was a fine gentleman." The woman pressed the widow's hand between her gloved ones. "I remember him so fondly from church gatherings."

Elizabeth doubted the woman had ever met Mr. Perkins. She'd seen her at three other funerals in recent weeks, always dressed impeccably in mourning clothes, always claiming some distant acquaintance with the deceased.

"I don't believe we've met," the widow said, wiping her eyes.

"Veronica Ashworth. My late father did business

with your husband some years ago." The lie came smoothly, accompanied by a sympathetic smile. "Will he be interred in the family plot?"

"Yes, alongside my parents in the north section."

"How fitting. And the service will be—?"

"This afternoon at four."

Elizabeth watched Veronica extract burial details with practised ease, asking questions that seemed born of polite interest but served a darker purpose. When the young woman moved away, she withdrew a small notebook from her reticule and made quick notes with a silver pencil.

"Who is that lady, Mother?" Elizabeth asked quietly.

Mary followed her gaze to Veronica, and a strange expression crossed her face, something between distaste and fear.

"No one you need concern yourself with," she replied, tightening her grip on Elizabeth's shoulder. "Come, we should pay our respects to Mrs. Perkins and then return home."

Later that evening, Elizabeth mentioned Veronica again over dinner. "The lady at the funeral today, Miss Ashworth, I've seen her at other funerals. Does she work for Father?"

The clatter of William's fork against his plate

broke the sudden silence. Mary's face paled, and she busied herself rearranging food she hadn't eaten.

"What makes you ask that?" William's tone was carefully neutral.

"She asks questions about burial arrangements and takes notes. Just like you told me, the business needs to know."

William exchanged a glance with Mary. "Miss Ashworth occasionally provides information useful to my associates. That's all."

"She's very pretty," Elizabeth observed innocently, watching her mother's reaction.

"That's quite enough, Elizabeth," Mary snapped. "Young ladies don't discuss such matters at dinner."

Elizabeth fell silent, but later that night, she heard her mother crying softly behind the closed bedroom door. She paused in the hallway, hand raised to knock but lowered it again without making her presence known. Some questions were better left unasked.

* * *

THE NEXT FUNERAL Elizabeth attended was for Mrs. Eleanor Whitmore, a neighbour who had succumbed to consumption. Once again, Veronica

Ashworth appeared among the mourners, this time claiming to be a distant cousin.

After the service, Elizabeth slipped away from her mother's side, determined to learn more about this mysterious woman who seemed connected to her father's business. She followed Veronica at a distance, trailing her through narrow streets as the afternoon shadows lengthened.

Veronica moved with purpose, consulting her notebook occasionally as she navigated London's maze-like lanes. Eventually, she turned into a small alley near the docks, not far from William's import office. Elizabeth hung back at the corner, peering cautiously around the brick wall.

Her father waited in the shadows, checking his pocket watch impatiently. When he spotted Veronica, his face transformed, lighting up with an expression Elizabeth had never seen before: naked adoration mixed with hunger.

"You're late," he said, but there was no anger in his voice.

"The service dragged on. The vicar was particularly verbose." Veronica stepped into his embrace without hesitation. "But I have excellent news. The Whitmore woman will be buried tomorrow at dusk, north corner of St. Mary's. No family to stand watch, and the groundskeeper can be bribed."

"Perfect." William's hands moved to Veronica's waist. "You're extraordinary, my dear. What would I do without you?"

"Earn considerably less money, I expect." Veronica laughed, a musical sound that carried clearly to Elizabeth's hiding place.

Then William kissed her; not the chaste kiss he gave Mary in public, but something passionate and desperate. Elizabeth shrank back, her chest tight with confusion and betrayal. This wasn't just business. Her father wasn't just employing Veronica to gather information. They were lovers.

"When can you leave her?" Veronica asked as they broke apart.

William sighed. "It's complicated. Mary is the mother of my child. And there are appearances to maintain."

"Appearances." Veronica's voice hardened. "You care more for how things look than how they are."

"That's not fair. You know what's at stake."

"I know I'm tired of hiding in alleys and pretending to be someone I'm not." Veronica pressed against him. "I want more, William."

"And you shall have it. I promise. Just be patient a little longer."

Elizabeth backed away, unable to bear any more. She ran blindly through the streets, tears blurring her vision as she ran through the alley abutting the docks, coming to a forced stop when she ran headlong into a bent-over man.

"Ah, child, what's the hurry then? Something chasing you, is it?" he asked with a heavy Irish accent.

"You...." Elizabeth sputtered, recognising the man as one of the regulars she had observed from her bedroom window at night over the years, meeting with her father to visit the cemeteries in the devilish hours when she was meant to be asleep in her bed. "You rob the graves with my father. I've seen you. You... you're a body snatcher."

He averted his eyes then, fussing with the brim of his cap as if he might tuck the truth underneath it. When he finally spoke again, his voice came rough and low, the way a man talks when he's been too long in the cold.

"I, young lady, am no such thing. I am a resurrectionist."

"You steal bodies from graves. You are a grave

robber. A body snatcher. I have read the Penny Dreadfuls and I know all about people like you, a sack-'em up man, a Sawbones' Collector.'"

"You're a smart one, huh. You want the truth, do you? About your father? About the digging?" He let out a breath that was not quite a sigh. "It's not the sort of information a girl like you ought to be chasing after. But since you're already halfway to knowing..."

He paused to glance over his shoulder before taking her in with eyes that weren't cruel, just tired.

"We take the dead, aye," he said plainly. "Graves that are freshly filled. Not all of them, mind you. We try to stick to the ones no one'll miss, or the ones buried too fine for anyone to notice if the earth's a little turned. It ain't pretty work. No one pretends it is. But it's not just ghoulishness, either, like your Penny Dreadfuls might lead you to believe. The bodies we take go to the surgeons, the real doctors. Those men who are trying to learn what's inside us, so maybe one day they'll know how to keep the rest of us alive."

He shifted his weight, glancing toward the shadows in the direction of the wall of the church from which she had just fled.

"You think it's vile, I can tell you do. I cannot blame you. But your father… he didn't fall into this because he wanted to. His business dried up, but not his debts. He had mouths to feed, same as any one of us. This pays. Sometimes, it pays more than honest work. And maybe, just maybe, some good will come of it. Even if it stinks of earth and rot and guilt."

He turned away from Elizabeth and started to walk away and then stopped. "Your father's not the devil, young miss. He just couldn't afford to be a gentleman any longer. He's not any one of those names you called me, either," he said, referring to the slang and euphemisms she had so proudly mentioned. "He is a resurrectionist."

As she watched him go, he disappeared, swallowed by the fog, and Elizabeth was left with just the cold and the silence, and something she could not quite describe. A sharp and sorrowful feeling lodged behind her ribs.

She realised her predicament and took off running, not slowing her pace until she found herself back at the church. Her mother stood by the gate, face tight with worry.

"Elizabeth! Where have you been? I've been frantic!"

"I'm sorry, Mother. I needed some air."

Mary studied her face. "You've been crying. What happened?"

Elizabeth opened her mouth, then closed it again, remembering her oath. What could she say? That her father was not only a grave robber but also unfaithful? That the woman who gathered information for his grim business was also his mistress?

"Nothing," she lied. "The funeral made me sad."

Mary didn't look convinced, but she took Elizabeth's hand and led her toward home, filling the silence with meaningless chatter about dinner plans and tomorrow's lessons. But Elizabeth noticed how her mother's eyes darted down the side streets as if expecting, or perhaps dreading, to see someone familiar.

That night, Elizabeth lay awake listening to the sounds of her home. The grandfather clock in the hall struck midnight, its deep chimes reverberating through the quiet house. Her father had not yet returned from his "business," and her mother's footsteps had paced the bedroom floor for hours before finally falling silent.

Just as Elizabeth was drifting toward sleep, raised voices from her parents' room jolted her awake. She slipped from her bed and crept to the wall that separated their rooms, pressing her ear against the flowered wallpaper.

"—don't care what excuses you make, William. I'm not a fool." Her mother's voice trembled with anger. "Half the neighbourhood has noticed your attention to that woman."

"Keep your voice down." William's tone was placating. "You're overreacting. Miss Ashworth is merely a business associate."

"A business associate who meets you in private? Who hangs on your every word at social gatherings? Do you think I don't see how you look at her?"

A heavy sigh. "Mary—"

"Don't lie to me! Not about this. I've accepted so much, William. I've closed my eyes to your midnight excursions. I've pretended not to know where our money comes from. I've smiled and played the respectable merchant's wife while you desecrate graves and consort with criminals."

"Everything I do is for this family. For our security and comfort."

"Is she for our family too?" Mary's voice broke. "Is

your pretty young informant part of providing for us?"

Silence stretched for several heartbeats.

"I never meant to hurt you," William said finally.

A bitter laugh. "How considerate."

"What would you have me do? Give up the business? Return to poverty? Watch you and Elizabeth starve or freeze? The import shop barely covers its own costs."

"I'm not asking you to give up the business. God help me, I've made my peace with that moral compromise." Mary's voice dropped lower, forcing Elizabeth to strain to hear. "But I won't be made a laughingstock by your infatuation with a girl barely older than our housemaid."

"She understands me. She doesn't flinch from the realities of what must be done."

"Because she has no morals to offend! While I—" Mary's voice caught. "I know what kind of man I married, William. I've always known, even before I understood exactly what you did in the night. But I never imagined it would come to this."

The sound of a door slamming ended the conversation. Heavy footsteps descended the stairs, followed by the front door closing with decisive force. Elizabeth crept to her window and watched her father by gaslight, stride away into the night, his figure soon swallowed by darkness.

From the next room came the muffled sound of her mother weeping. Elizabeth wanted to go to her, to offer comfort, but what could she say? They were both trapped by William's choices: Mary by marriage and financial dependence, Elizabeth by her oath and fear of the workhouse.

Elizabeth returned to bed, pulling the covers tight around her shoulders against a chill that had nothing to do with the temperature. Her mother knew everything about the grave robbing, the affair, yet chose to remain silent rather than risk losing her comfortable life. Another kind of accomplice.

In the darkness of her bedroom, Elizabeth faced a terrible truth: both her parents had sacrificed their principles for security and comfort. Both had chosen to look away from unpleasant realities when convenient. And both expected her to do the same.

She touched the silver locket at her throat, the price of her silence. At ten years old, Elizabeth understood she stood at a crossroads. She could follow her parents' example, closing her eyes to wrongdoing for the sake of comfort. Or she could find another path, though what that might be, she couldn't yet imagine.

The house settled into silence broken only by the distant sounds of London at night and her mother's gradually subsiding tears. Elizabeth lay awake until dawn, watching shadows move across her ceiling and wondering what other secrets lurked behind the respectable facade of her childhood home.

CHAPTER 3

The newspaper lay open on the breakfast table, the bold headline staring up at Elizabeth like an accusation: "Respectable Merchant Revealed as Ghoulish Body Snatcher." Below it, a crude illustration showed men being apprehended in a cemetery, shovels in hand and a half-exposed coffin at their feet. Though the drawing was inexact, Elizabeth recognised her father's distinctive profile among the captured men.

"Take that away," Mary ordered the maid, her voice brittle as she gestured to the offending paper. "And draw the curtains tighter. I can still see people gathering outside."

Elizabeth moved to the window, peering through

a narrow gap in the heavy drapes. A small crowd had formed on the street, pointing at their house and speaking behind raised hands. Mrs. Pemberton from the charitable ladies' society stood among them, her face pinched with righteous disgust as she held forth to her companions.

"They're still there," Elizabeth reported, letting the curtain fall back into place. "More than before."

"Vultures," Mary whispered, pressing her handkerchief to bloodless lips. "After all we've contributed to neighbourhood causes. All the times we've hosted their dreary gatherings."

Elizabeth said nothing. At twelve years old, she understood the hypocrisy of her mother's indignation. The charitable donations, the social gatherings, the respectable façade, all purchased with profits from violated graves. The very neighbour now gossiping outside their door had unknowingly sipped tea bought with money from their own relatives' corpses.

"When will Father come home?" she asked instead.

Mary's laugh held no humour. "Not soon. The magistrate denied bail. Your father will remain in Newgate until his case is heard."

"How long?"

"Weeks. Perhaps months." Mary's hand trembled as she poured herself another cup of tea. "We must manage as best we can until then."

Elizabeth nodded, watching her mother's trembling hands and too-bright eyes. She recognised the signs of the laudanum drops Mary had increasingly relied upon since discovering William's affair with Veronica. Now, with public disgrace added to private betrayal, Elizabeth wondered if her mother would disappear entirely into the cloudy comfort of the brown medicine bottle.

A sharp rap at the front door made them both start. The maid appeared in the doorway, her expression anxious.

"It's Mr. Hargreaves from the butcher's shop, ma'am. Says he needs to speak with you about the account."

Mary closed her eyes briefly. "Tell him I'm indisposed."

"He was most insistent, ma'am. Says he can't extend credit any further without... without payment in full of the existing balance."

The first of many such visits, Elizabeth suspected. With William in prison and their social standing destroyed, how long before the comfortable life they'd known collapsed entirely?

* * *

"THE GHOUL'S DAUGHTER! The ghoul's daughter!"

The children's taunts followed Elizabeth across the school yard, their sing-song voices carrying in the spring air. She kept her head high, clutching her books to her chest like armour, though her cheeks burned with humiliation.

"Did your father bring you a dead man's finger for your birthday, Lizzie Flanders?"

"Does he make you kiss the corpses goodnight?"

A foot thrust into her path sent Elizabeth sprawling onto the gravel. Her books were scattered, and her palms stung where they scraped against the rough ground. Laughter erupted around her as she struggled to her knees.

"Careful, everyone! Don't touch her! Grave dirt might rub off!"

Elizabeth gathered her books without looking up, years of practised composure keeping her tears at bay. Only when a shadow fell across her did she raise her eyes.

Miss Thornton, her mathematics teacher, stood over her with an expression caught between duty and distaste. "That's enough," she called to the circling children, though her rebuke lacked conviction. "Return to your classes immediately."

The children dispersed, still giggling. Miss Thornton made no move to help Elizabeth collect her remaining books.

"You should clean yourself up before afternoon lessons, Miss Flanders." Her tone was cool, professional. "Your appearance is... unsuitable."

Elizabeth nodded, watching the teacher stride away. Even the adults who should protect her had withdrawn their sympathy. In the eight weeks since her father's arrest, she had learned how quickly respectability could evaporate, how conditional the world's kindness truly was.

In the girls' washroom, Elizabeth dabbed at her torn stockings and scraped hands. The face that looked back from the small mirror was thinner than it had been two months ago, with shadows under the eyes that spoke of sleepless nights and constant vigilance. Her once-neat school uniform showed signs of repeated mending, the result of daily attacks that tore buttons and ripped seams.

She would need to take a different route home

today. Yesterday, a group of boys had followed her for three streets, throwing horse dung and shouting obscenities about her father. The day before, Mrs. Winters from the bakery had refused to sell her bread, claiming they didn't serve "families of ghouls."

Elizabeth straightened her collar, smoothed her hair, and prepared to face the afternoon lessons. The mathematics of survival was becoming her most important subject: how to navigate a world that had decided she was tainted by her father's crimes.

* * *

The stench hit Elizabeth first: a miasma of unwashed bodies, human waste, and despair that seemed to cling to the very stones of Newgate Prison. She pressed a handkerchief to her nose as the guard led her through narrow corridors toward the common holding area where her father awaited.

"Ten minutes," the guard grunted, unlocking a heavy door. "No passing of items without inspection."

The cell beyond was crowded with men in various states of dishevelment. Some sprawled on filthy straw pallets; others huddled in small groups, speaking in low voices that ceased abruptly when the door opened. In the far corner, William Flanders sat on a wooden stool, his once-immaculate clothing now stained and wrinkled.

"Elizabeth." He rose quickly, crossing to embrace her. "My dear girl."

She allowed the embrace, though the unfamiliar smell of her father's sweat and dirt rather than his usual cologne made her stomach turn. His face was gaunt, with several days' growth of beard shadowing his jaw, and a yellowing bruise marked his left cheekbone.

"Mother sends her regards," Elizabeth said, the formal phrase sounding hollow in this desperate place. In truth, Mary had refused to visit, claiming illness, but actually unwilling to face the public humiliation of being seen entering the prison.

"How is she managing?" William asked, leading Elizabeth to his corner where they might speak with some small privacy.

"As well as can be expected. The tradesmen are demanding immediate payment of accounts. Mother has sold some jewellery to cover immediate expenses."

William's expression darkened. "Vultures. The moment a man faces difficulty, they circle. And our neighbour's? Our friends?"

Elizabeth hesitated, unwilling to add to his burdens. "They've been... distant."

"You mean they've abandoned us." William laughed bitterly. "Fair-weather friends, the lot of them. Happy enough to attend our dinner parties and accept our charitable donations, but quick to turn when fortunes change."

A rough-looking man with a scar bisecting his left eyebrow approached, eyeing Elizabeth with undisguised curiosity. "This your daughter, Flanders? Pretty little thing."

William nodded. "Elizabeth, meet Mr. Morris. One of my... business associates."

Morris grinned, revealing several missing teeth. "Your pa's been educating us on the finer points of the resurrection trade. Quite the expert, he is. Never knew there was so much science to it."

Elizabeth stared at the man, disturbed by his casual reference to grave robbing as a trade with finer points.

"It's all about knowing which specimens command the best prices," William explained, as if discussing the import of spices rather than stolen corpses. "The medical schools pay premium rates for unusual conditions or specific age groups. It's simply a matter of supply and demand."

"And your pa knows all the right people," Morris added. "Doctors, professors, them fancy medical school fellows. Not like us small-timers who have to work through middlemen."

Elizabeth listened in growing horror as her father introduced other cellmates: Harrison, who specialised in cemetery security systems, Jenkins, whose cousin worked at the morgue, and Blackwood, who crafted specialised tools for quick, quiet excavation. These weren't ashamed criminals awaiting punishment; they were professionals discussing their craft, temporarily inconvenienced by the law.

"The mistake was working too close to the fashionable cemeteries," William explained, his voice taking on the instructional tone he once used for teaching Elizabeth arithmetic. "The new burial grounds have better security, but they also have wealthier clientele, which means better-constructed coffins and more valuable specimens. It's a calculated risk."

"Father," Elizabeth interrupted, unable to bear more, "when will you come home?"

William's expression softened. "Soon, my dear. My solicitor believes they'll sentence me to two months with hard labour. With time already served,

I should return within a few weeks."

"And then?"

"And then we rebuild." His eyes hardened with determination. "This is merely a setback, not an end. I've made valuable connections here." He gestured around the cell. "Men with skills and knowledge that will prove useful."

Elizabeth realised with a sinking heart that her father had no intention of abandoning his criminal activities. Prison had not prompted reflection or remorse, only more careful planning.

"Your ten minutes are up," the guard called, rattling his keys.

William embraced her again, whispering in her ear, "Tell your mother to contact Veronica. She knows where certain items are stored that will help with expenses until my return."

The name sent a chill through Elizabeth. Of course, Veronica would remain in their lives, perhaps now more openly than before.

"Be brave, my girl," William said, releasing her. "This world respects strength and cleverness above all. Remember that."

Elizabeth nodded automatically, though the lesson seemed a poor one to impart to a child. As the guard led her back through the corridors, she tried to reconcile the diminished man in the cell with the father she had known and wondered which was the true William Flanders.

* * *

WILLIAM'S RETURN brought no relief to the Flanders household. He arrived home on a grey Tuesday afternoon, thinner and harder than when he'd left, with a coldness in his eyes that hadn't been there before. Prison had stripped away the veneer of gentility, revealing the calculating criminal beneath.

"The business resumes tonight," he announced over dinner, not bothering to lower his voice though the maid was clearing the table. "I've arranged meetings with my most reliable associates."

"William, please," Mary whispered, glancing nervously at the servant. "Perhaps we might discuss this privately?"

He dismissed her concern with a wave. "Why bother with pretence now? Our standing is already compromised. Better to focus on rebuilding our finances than maintaining appearances for neighbours who've shown their true colours."

Within days, the house Elizabeth had once known was transformed. Rough men arrived at all hours, no longer slinking through the back entrance but boldly using the front door. The drawing room where Mary had once hosted charitable society meetings became a planning centre for grave robbing operations, with maps of cemeteries spread across tables and detailed lists of recent burials discussed openly.

William recruited new diggers, bribed additional cemetery workers, and cultivated fresh contacts at medical schools hungry for specimens. His approach was more aggressive, more organised, and entirely without the secrecy that had previously cloaked their family life.

"The mistake wasn't getting caught," he explained to a group of associates while Elizabeth sat quietly in the corner, supposedly working on her needlepoint but actually absorbing every word. "The mistake was thinking small. Working alone. Relying on stealth rather than strategy."

Elizabeth watched her father map out territories, assign teams to different burial grounds, and calculate profits with cold precision. The charming businessman who had once maintained a legitimate front had vanished, to be replaced by a criminal mastermind who spoke of corpses as commodities and graves as resources to be harvested.

Mary retreated further into laudanum-induced fog, taking meals in her room and emerging only when absolutely necessary. The household staff dwindled as servants gave notice, unwilling to remain in a home now openly associated with grave robbing. Only Mrs. Perkins, the cook and Agnes, the housemaid, remained, both too old or desperate to seek positions elsewhere.

Elizabeth continued attending school, though the daily torments made learning nearly impossible. Her former friends had abandoned her entirely, and teachers made little effort to hide their disapproval. Only her natural intelligence and stubborn determination kept her from academic failure.

"Why must I still go?" she asked her father after a particularly brutal day left her with a torn skirt and ink dumped over her copybooks. "No one wants me there."

William looked up from the cemetery map he was studying. "Education is power, Elizabeth. Those who shun you now may work for you someday, if you're clever enough. Besides," he added with a cold smile, "it maintains the fiction that we still care about respectability. Useful for certain business contacts."

Elizabeth nodded, understanding that "certain

business contacts" meant the doctors and medical professors who still preferred to pretend they weren't dealing with criminals. Even in disgrace, appearances mattered, just in different ways than before.

Life had taken on many kinds of different since her father's change in morality.

Changes...

The most significant change came with Veronica's elevated position in the household. No longer a secret mistress glimpsed in shadowy alleys, she now visited openly, sweeping into the house in fashionable gowns that made Mary's dated dresses seem shabby by comparison.

"The south section of Highgate had three burials yesterday," Veronica announced one evening, spreading her notes across the dining table where Mary had once served tea to society ladies. "Two elderly men, unremarkable specimens, but also a woman of twenty-five who died in childbirth. Excellent anatomical subject. St. Bartholomew's would pay handsomely."

William nodded approvingly. "Excellent work, my dear. Harrison can lead the expedition tonight."

Elizabeth, seated in the corner with a book she wasn't reading, watched Veronica direct operations with the confidence of a general. At nineteen, she possessed a cold intelligence that made her valuable to William's business and dangerous to anyone who opposed her.

"The groundskeeper has been replaced," Veronica continued. "The new man seems amenable to arrangement but requires a higher payment than his predecessor."

"Offer him five pounds for the first month, with an increase to seven if he proves reliable." William turned to one of his men. "Morris, you'll make the approach. You have a common touch that puts these fellows at ease."

Mary appeared in the doorway, her face pale and her movements unsteady. "William, I need to speak with you regarding household accounts."

Veronica barely glanced at her. "We're in the middle of business matters, Mrs. Flanders. Perhaps later?"

The casual dismissal hung in the air like a slap. Mary's fingers tightened on the doorframe, but she lacked the strength, whether physical or emotional or both, to challenge the younger woman who had usurped her position in her own home.

"Of course," she murmured, withdrawing without meeting Elizabeth's eyes.

Later that night, Elizabeth found her mother sitting alone in her bedroom, staring at her reflection in the vanity mirror. The once-beautiful woman looked years older than her thirty years, with dull hair and hollow cheeks.

"Are you well, Mother?" Elizabeth asked, though the answer was obvious.

Mary's laugh held no humour. "What a question, child. No, I am not well. None of us is well." She picked up her hairbrush but set it down again without using it. "I should have taken you away when your father was first arrested. Found positions as governesses or companions. Anything to escape this... this mockery of a home."

"We could still leave," Elizabeth suggested, though she knew it was an empty offer.

"And go where? With what money?" Mary shook her head. "The world is unkind to women without resources or protection. At least here we have a roof and food, however tainted the source." She reached for the laudanum bottle on her dressing table. "Sometimes oblivion is the only escape available."

Elizabeth watched her mother measure the brown liquid into a glass, diluting it with water before drinking. The familiar ritual had become more frequent, the doses larger, as Veronica's presence in the house grew more dominant.

"She's destroying us," Elizabeth said quietly.

Mary didn't pretend to misunderstand. "No, child. Your father destroyed us when he chose his criminal path. Veronica is merely the beneficiary of our collapse." She set down the empty glass. "Go to bed, Elizabeth. Tomorrow will be difficult enough without adding exhaustion."

Elizabeth obeyed, but sleep eluded her as voices drifted up from below, William and Veronica planning the next night's operations, their tones intimate and exclusive. In the adjacent room, she heard her mother's muffled weeping gradually subside as the laudanum took effect.

The Flanders home had become a place of shadows and secrets even darker than before, with Elizabeth caught between her father's criminal ambitions, her mother's deterioration, and Veronica's cold calculation. Each day pulled her further from the possibility of a normal, respectable life.

* * *

"You're coming with us tonight."

Elizabeth looked up from her studies, startled by

her father's announcement. Two years had passed since she'd discovered the hidden ledgers, and in that time, she'd maintained a careful distance from the actual operations of his business. Knowledge without participation had been her compromise with conscience.

"I don't understand."

William smiled, but the expression didn't warm his eyes. "It's time you learned the practical side of our enterprise. You're twelve now, old enough to contribute."

"As what?" Elizabeth asked, though she already feared the answer.

"A lookout, initially. Children attract less suspicion than adults lingering near cemeteries." He laid a hand on her shoulder. "You've benefited from this business your entire life, Elizabeth. The food you eat, the clothes you wear, the books you read, all paid for by my work. It's only fair you understand exactly what that entails."

Elizabeth wanted to refuse, to lock herself in her room and pretend this conversation had never happened. But she recognised the implacable resolve in her father's expression. This wasn't a request.

"When?" she asked, resignation replacing resistance.

"Tonight. Wear dark clothing, nothing that reflects light. And practical shoes; the ground will be damp."

At dusk, Elizabeth found herself walking beside her father toward Brompton Cemetery, her heart pounding so loudly she was certain passersby must hear it. William carried a small bag containing tools whose purpose she tried not to contemplate. Two of his associates, Morris and a newer man called Jenks, walked several paces ahead, posing as ordinary labourers heading home after work.

"Remember," William instructed quietly, "your job is to watch the main path. If anyone approaches, particularly cemetery guards or police, you are to whistle once, sharply, like this." He demonstrated a piercing signal. "Then retreat to the oak tree by the north wall and wait."

Elizabeth nodded, her throat too dry for speech. The cemetery gates loomed ahead, their wrought iron scrollwork resembling skeletal hands in the fading light. Morris and Jenks slipped inside through a service entrance, while William led Elizabeth along the perimeter wall to a section where age had weakened the stone.

"Up you go," he said, lacing his fingers to create a step for her. "I'll be right behind you."

The wall was cold and rough beneath her palms as she scrambled over, dropping down into the cemetery grounds with a soft thud. All around, gravestones stretched in orderly rows, their marble and granite surfaces ghostly in the gathering darkness. The smell of damp earth and decaying flowers filled her nostrils.

William landed beside her with practised ease, immediately orienting himself among the markers. "This way," he whispered, leading her along a narrow path between elaborate family vaults.

They met Morris and Jenks beside a fresh grave, the turned earth still dark against the surrounding grass. A simple wooden marker bore the name "Emily Watson, 1830-1850, Beloved Daughter."

"Young female, no obvious disease," Morris reported. "Buried yesterday afternoon. Family from out of town, already departed London. No watchers expected."

William nodded approvingly. "Perfect. Elizabeth, take position by that angel monument. You can see the main path from there. Remember the signal if anyone comes."

Elizabeth moved numbly to her assigned post, trying not to look as the men produced shovels from their bags and began systematically removing earth from the grave. The sound of metal cutting into soil seemed unnaturally loud in the quiet cemetery, though she knew the men were working as silently as possible.

Time stretched as Elizabeth kept vigil, every distant sound making her heart race. A cat prowling among the tombstones. An owl calling from a nearby tree. The rumble of a carriage on the street beyond the wall. Each noise momentarily froze the diggers until they determined no threat existed.

After what seemed like hours but might have been only forty minutes, she heard a dull thud followed by Morris's hushed voice: "Hit the coffin."

Elizabeth closed her eyes, unwilling to witness what came next, but her father's sharp command forced them open again.

"Elizabeth. Come here."

She approached reluctantly, keeping her gaze fixed on her father's face rather than the open grave.

"Look," William instructed, gesturing downward. "This is our business. No point averting your eyes from reality."

Slowly, Elizabeth lowered her gaze. The men had cleared the earth from the coffin lid and pried it open with specialised tools. Inside lay the body of a young woman in a white burial dress, her face peaceful as if sleeping. In death, she looked hardly older than Elizabeth herself.

"A perfect specimen," William commented clinically. "No visible decomposition, excellent musculature for anatomical study. St. Bartholomew's will pay fifteen pounds, possibly more."

Elizabeth swallowed hard against rising nausea. This was someone's daughter, someone's beloved Emily, now discussed like merchandise at a market.

"Help Morris with the sack," William directed. "Jenks and I will extract the specimen."

Bile rose in Elizabeth's throat, but she forced herself to hold the canvas bag open as the men carefully lifted the body from its coffin. The dead woman's arm brushed against Elizabeth's hand, cold, waxy, yet still horribly human. She bit her lip until she tasted blood, focusing on that small pain to block out the larger horror.

Once the body was secured in the sack, the men worked quickly to replace the coffin lid and refill the grave. Within twenty minutes, the site looked undisturbed except for the slightly mounded earth that might be attributed to natural settling.

"Well done," William said as they made their way back toward the cemetery wall. "A clean operation. Your first of many, Elizabeth."

She remained silent, concentrating on placing one foot before the other, on breathing in and out, on not vomiting or screaming or collapsing under the weight of what she had witnessed; what she had helped accomplish.

Later, after the "specimen" had been delivered to a back entrance of St. Bartholomew's Hospital and payment received, William pressed a gold sovereign into Elizabeth's palm.

"Your share," he said with evident pride. "You've earned it."

The coin felt impossibly heavy in her hand, its gleaming surface reflecting the gas lamps of the street where they stood. Blood money. Death money. The price of her soul.

"Thank you, Father," she whispered, because no other response was possible.

As they walked home through London's dark streets, Elizabeth clutched the sovereign in her pocket and understood that something fundamental had changed. She was no longer merely the daughter of a criminal, no longer simply aware of wrongs committed by others. She had crossed from unwilling knowledge into active participation, from innocence into complicity.

The gold burned against her palm like a brand,

marking her as what the neighbourhood children had already named her: the ghoul's daughter. Only now the title was earned, not merely inherited. And Elizabeth wondered, with a hollowness that seemed to consume her from within, whether there could ever be a path back to the person she might have been.

CHAPTER 4

The porcelain teacup rattled against its saucer as Mary Flanders' hand shook. She set it down carefully, a faint grimace crossing her face as another spasm of pain gripped her stomach.

"Mother?" Elizabeth studied her mother's pallid complexion, noting the dark circles beneath her eyes and the slight yellowish tinge to her skin. "Shall I call for Dr. Morrison again?"

"No need to trouble him." Mary attempted a smile that didn't reach her eyes. "It's merely a touch of indigestion."

Elizabeth knew better. For weeks now, her mother had suffered these episodes of violent nausea, stabbing abdominal pains, and a gradual wasting that had left her gowns hanging loosely on her once-elegant frame. Dr. Morrison had visited three times already, each time departing with a furrowed brow and a new, ineffective tonic.

"Perhaps some fresh air would help." Elizabeth moved to open the drawing room curtains, but Mary shook her head sharply.

"The light hurts my eyes today." She reached for her teacup again, her fingers trembling so badly that amber liquid sloshed over the rim. "Where is Veronica? She promised to bring more of her herbal tea. It's the only thing that offers any relief."

As if summoned by the mention of her name, Veronica appeared in the doorway, carrying a small silver tray with a steaming teapot. At nineteen, she had grown more beautiful and more confident in her position within the household. Her dark hair was arranged fashionably, her violet eyes bright with intelligence, her slender figure shown to advantage in a well-fitted day dress of deep burgundy.

"Here we are, Mrs. Flanders," she announced cheerfully. "Grandmother's special blend. Chamomile for soothing, peppermint for digestion, and a few other herbs known only to the women in my family." She poured a cup with practised grace.

"Drink it while it's hot, that's when the medicinal properties are strongest."

Mary accepted the cup gratefully. "You're too kind, looking after a tiresome invalid when you could be helping William with more important matters."

"Nonsense," Veronica replied, her smile revealing perfect teeth. "Your comfort is of utmost importance to William, which makes it important to me." She glanced at Elizabeth, her expression cooling slightly. "Elizabeth, dear, perhaps you could fetch your mother's shawl? She seems chilled."

It wasn't a request but a dismissal. Elizabeth hesitated, reluctant to leave her mother alone with Veronica, but Mary nodded in agreement.

"Yes, the blue one, please. It's in my bedroom."

Elizabeth departed unwillingly, pausing in the hallway to glance back. Through the partially open door, she watched Veronica lean close to Mary, speaking too softly for Elizabeth to hear. Whatever she said made Mary drink deeply from the cup, grimacing at the bitter taste.

By the time Elizabeth returned with the shawl, her mother was already showing the familiar pattern of a brief period of seeming improvement followed by intensified symptoms. Her face had gained a sheen of sweat, and her breathing had quickened.

"I think I shall rest now," Mary murmured, allowing Elizabeth to drape the shawl around her shoulders. "The tea always makes me rather drowsy."

"I'll help you to your room," Elizabeth offered, shooting a suspicious glance at Veronica.

"I can manage." Mary rose unsteadily, waving away assistance. "You have your studies to attend to."

As her mother left the room, Elizabeth noticed something that sent a chill through her body. The teacup Mary had been using before Veronica arrived, the one containing ordinary breakfast tea, sat abandoned on the side table. Despite Mary's supposedly delicate stomach, she had consumed Veronica's special brew completely, leaving only a residue of dark sediment at the bottom of the cup.

Veronica gathered the tea things, humming softly to herself, seemingly oblivious to Elizabeth's scrutiny. But as she turned to leave, she caught Elizabeth's eye and held it for a moment. Something in that violet gaze, a cold calculation, a silent warning, made Elizabeth's heart thump painfully against her ribs.

"Your mother is fortunate to have my care,"

Veronica said quietly. "Some illnesses respond only to very particular treatments."

The words hung in the air between them, innocent on the surface but carrying an undercurrent that made Elizabeth's mouth go dry. By the time she thought to respond, Veronica had already glided from the room, taking the evidence of her "special blend" with her.

Elizabeth waited until the house settled into afternoon quiet before investigating Veronica's "medicinal herbs." With William at his office and her mother resting after another bout of violent illness, she slipped into the conservatory where Veronica had established her small botanical domain.

The glass-walled room bloomed with plants of all descriptions. In the centre, visible to any visitor, grew recognisable healing herbs: chamomile with its daisy-like flowers, mint spreading enthusiastically in its container, lavender releasing its calming scent when brushed. These were the plants Veronica proudly displayed when explaining her "grandmother's remedies" to William or visitors.

But Elizabeth's attention focused on the less prominent specimens tucked against the back wall, partially hidden behind larger pots. Here grew plants she recognised from her father's medical books as plants no household should cultivate without good reason.

Foxglove, with its tall spires of purple-pink bells, beautiful but containing digitalis that could stop a heart. Delicate white flowers of hemlock rising above lacy leaves, capable of paralysing a victim from the feet upward until breathing ceased. Oleander with its attractive pink blooms that conceal enough poison in a single leaf to kill a child.

Elizabeth examined these deadly specimens with growing horror. Unlike the somewhat haphazard arrangement of the medicinal herbs, these plants were meticulously tended, soil perfectly moist, dead leaves removed, positions adjusted for optimal light. Veronica lavished particular care on her poisons.

Behind a large fern, Elizabeth discovered a small wooden box. She hesitated, glancing toward the door, then carefully lifted the lid. Inside lay a leather-bound notebook similar to her father's business ledgers but smaller and more feminine in its proportions. She opened it to find pages of elegant handwriting. Veronica's distinctive script.

The contents chilled her blood. Detailed notes on various toxins, their properties, symptoms they produce, and methods of administration. Foxglove: "Causes vomiting, abdominal pain, visual disturbances, and eventual heart failure. Best administered gradually to mimic natural disease. Easily masked in bitter tea."

Elizabeth turned the pages with trembling fingers. Veronica had created a poisoner's handbook, complete with observations from what appeared to be actual cases:

"Subject A: Female, 62, robust health. Initial dose produced mild symptoms only. Increased concentration resulted in desired effect within three weeks. Death attributed to heart weakness by physician."

"Subject B: Female, 58, previous digestive complaints. Ideal candidate as symptoms easily attributed to existing condition. Complete success in 18 days. Substantial inheritance secured through prior cultivation of friendship."

The methodical documentation continued across multiple pages, each entry representing a life systematically extinguished. Elizabeth realised she was looking at evidence of multiple murders, cold-blooded, calculated, and profitable.

A notation on the final page caught her eye: "M.F.: Female, 30, weakened by emotional distress and laudanum use. Particularly susceptible to cumulative effects. Estimated completion: 6-8 weeks from initial dose. Proceeding carefully to avoid suspicion."

M.F. Mary Flanders.

Elizabeth nearly dropped the notebook. Her mother wasn't suffering from a mysterious illness, she was being systematically poisoned by Veronica. And according to this timeline, the process had begun shortly after William's return from prison.

The sound of the conservatory door opening sent Elizabeth scrambling to replace the notebook and retreat behind a large palm. Veronica entered, carrying a small basket and pruning shears. She moved directly to her poisonous collection, examining each plant with a proprietor's pride before carefully snipping leaves and flowers from several specimens.

"Foxglove for the heart, hemlock for the nerves," she murmured to herself, placing each cutting in her basket. "Poor Mrs. Flanders, suffering so. But not for much longer."

Elizabeth pressed her hand against her mouth to stifle a gasp. She remained frozen behind the palm until Veronica departed, then fled the conservatory, her mind racing with the terrible knowledge she'd acquired.

Her mother was being murdered before her eyes, and the killer lived in their home, slept under their roof, and enjoyed her father's complete trust and affection.

* * *

"WHO IS MRS. ADELAIDE WHITMORE?" Elizabeth asked her father at breakfast the following morning. Mary was absent, too ill to leave her bed.

William looked up from his newspaper with mild surprise. "A widow who lives in Belgravia. Quite wealthy, I believe. Why do you ask?"

"I overheard Veronica mentioning her name." Elizabeth kept her tone casual, though her heart raced. "She seemed quite interested in the lady's health."

"Ah, yes. Veronica does charitable work with elderly widows through St. Michael's Church." William smiled proudly. "She has a gift for bringing comfort to the lonely. Mrs. Whitmore has no family, I understand, and has grown quite attached to Veronica's visits."

Elizabeth nodded thoughtfully. "How kind of her to spend time with old women when she could be doing more exciting things."

"That's our Veronica, always thinking of others."

William returned to his newspaper, the matter closed in his mind.

But Elizabeth had found her next step. If Veronica was indeed targeting wealthy, isolated widows as her notebook suggested, then Mrs. Adelaide Whitmore might be her current victim. And unlike Mary, who was already deep in the poisoning process, Mrs. Whitmore might still be saved.

For the next week, Elizabeth carefully tracked Veronica's movements. Three afternoons, she followed her to a handsome townhouse in Belgravia, watching from across the street as Veronica was admitted like a favoured guest. On the third visit, she carried a small basket similar to the one she'd used in the conservatory, undoubtedly containing her "special tea."

On her fourth expedition, Elizabeth gathered her courage and approached the house directly. She knocked on the servant's entrance, where a tired-looking maid answered.

"I've a message for Mrs. Whitmore," Elizabeth said, adopting the manner of a tradesman's daughter. "From the church committee."

The maid frowned. "The mistress isn't receiving messages today. She's taken quite ill."

"What sort of illness?" Elizabeth asked, her stomach tightening with dread.

"Started with stomach upsets, poor lady. Now she can hardly keep anything down and suffers terrible pains." The maid lowered her voice. "The doctor's been twice this week, but his medicines don't help. Only Miss Ashworth's special teas seem to offer any relief, though they make the mistress dreadfully sleepy afterwards."

The familiar pattern confirmed Elizabeth's worst fears. "When did she first become ill?"

"About three weeks past, just after Miss Ashworth began visiting regularly." The maid's eyes narrowed suddenly. "Who did you say you were from?"

"St. Michael's Church," Elizabeth replied quickly. "Please tell Mrs. Whitmore we're praying for her swift recovery."

She hurried away before the maid could ask more questions. Three weeks into the poisoning process, according to Veronica's notebook, Mrs. Whitmore might have only days remaining before the final, fatal dose was administered.

Elizabeth considered her options as she walked home through London's busy streets. She could try to warn Mrs. Whitmore directly, but a bedridden woman might not believe accusations from a strange child against her trusted companion. She could approach the authorities, but what evidence did she have beyond a glimpse of a notebook she couldn't produce?

Her father was the logical choice; surely even his infatuation with Veronica would waver if he understood she was a systematic poisoner. But would he believe his daughter over his beloved?

She had to try.

* * *

"FATHER, I need to speak with you." Elizabeth stood in the doorway of William's study, her hands clasped tightly to stop their trembling. "It's important."

William glanced up from his desk, where cemetery maps and payment records lay spread before him. "Can it wait, my dear? I'm rather busy with tomorrow's operations."

"It's about Veronica."

Something in her tone caught his attention. He set down his pen and gestured to the chair opposite his desk. "What about her?"

Elizabeth took a deep breath. "I believe she's poisoning Mother."

William's expression remained unchanged for several heartbeats, then his eyebrows rose in disbelief. "What nonsense is this?"

"It's not nonsense. Mother's symptoms began shortly after Veronica started preparing her 'special teas.' I've seen Veronica's collection of poisonous plants in the conservatory: foxglove, hemlock, oleander. And I found her notebook with detailed records of poisoning methods."

"You went through Veronica's private possessions?" William's voice hardened.

"I had to. Mother grows worse every day, and the pattern matches exactly what Veronica has done before. She targets vulnerable women, gains their trust, then poisons them slowly to make it appear natural."

"This is absurd." William stood abruptly. "Your mother suffers from a nervous condition, exacerbated by the difficulties our family has faced. Veronica has been nothing but kind, preparing herbal remedies to ease her discomfort."

"Remedies that make her worse!" Elizabeth's voice rose with frustration. "And she's doing the same to Mrs. Whitmore, a wealthy widow who's now deathly ill after three weeks of Veronica's 'care.'"

"Enough!" William slammed his palm against the desk. "I won't listen to these jealous fabrications."

"Jealous?" Elizabeth stared at her father in disbelief.

"Yes, jealous. You've resented Veronica since she entered our lives because she received attention you felt entitled to. But this—" he gestured dismissively, "—this fantasy of poisoning goes beyond childish pique into malicious slander."

"It's not fantasy! I've seen the evidence with my own eyes. Veronica is a murderer, and Mother will be her next victim if we don't stop her!"

William's face darkened with anger. "Go to your room, Elizabeth. We'll discuss your punishment for these accusations later."

"You're blind where she's concerned," Elizabeth whispered, tears welling in her eyes. "She's manipulated you completely."

"Room. Now." William pointed to the door, his expression brooking no further argument.

Elizabeth retreated, her last hope crumbling. As she climbed the stairs to her bedroom, a soft voice stopped her on the landing.

"Such an imaginative child."

Veronica stood in the shadows of the hallway, her beautiful face composed in an expression of amused contempt. She moved closer, her skirts rustling softly against the carpet.

"Did you really think he would believe you over me?" she asked, her voice barely above a whisper. "William sees what he wishes to see, a devoted companion who understands his ambitions rather than a judgmental wife who flinches at his business."

"You're killing my mother," Elizabeth said flatly.

"I'm accelerating the inevitable. Your mother was already killing herself with laudanum and misery." Veronica's violet eyes gleamed in the dim light. "But you... You're more troublesome than I anticipated. Watching, following, investigating. So like your father in your determination but lacking his blindness where pretty faces are concerned."

She reached out to touch Elizabeth's cheek, her fingers cold against the girl's skin. Elizabeth jerked away, pressing herself against the bannister.

"Don't worry about Mrs. Whitmore," Veronica continued conversationally. "Her suffering will end soon. As for your mother, well, some illnesses progress faster than others. It depends on the patient's constitution." She smiled, revealing perfect white teeth. "And on how much of a nuisance their family becomes."

The threat hung in the air between them, clear despite its indirect phrasing.

"If anything happens to Mother suddenly, I'll tell everyone what you've done," Elizabeth warned, her voice steadier than she felt.

"Who would believe you? The disturbed daughter of a grave robber, known for telling tales?" Veronica laughed softly. "Besides, grief affects young minds in strange ways. After losing your mother, you might suffer a tragic accident yourself. William would be devastated, of course, but I would comfort him."

She moved past Elizabeth, the scent of her perfume, lilies and something sharper beneath, lingering in the air.

"Sweet dreams, Elizabeth," she called over her shoulder. "Do try that new tea I left in your room. It's a special blend."

Elizabeth remained frozen on the landing long after Veronica disappeared down the corridor. The conversation had confirmed her worst fears; Veronica was not only a poisoner but had now marked Elizabeth herself as a target. With her father bewitched and her mother incapacitated, she had no protectors left in the household that had once been her haven.

That night, she poured Veronica's "special blend"

into the chamber pot and locked her bedroom door, pushing a chair beneath the handle for good measure. But as she lay awake in the darkness, listening to the unfamiliar sounds of the house settling, Elizabeth knew that locks and vigilance offered only temporary security.

Veronica had murdered before and would murder again. Mary Flanders would soon join the list of victims in that meticulous notebook, followed perhaps by Mrs. Whitmore, and eventually, when she became too troublesome to tolerate, Elizabeth herself.

Unless she found a way to stop the beautiful poisoner who had invaded their home and destroyed their family from within.

Three days later, Elizabeth stood across the street from Mrs. Whitmore's house, watching as a doctor emerged, shaking his head solemnly. Behind him, a maid wept into her apron. Even from a distance, the message was clear: the wealthy widow had succumbed to her mysterious illness.

Elizabeth's chest tightened with guilt and grief. She had failed to save Mrs. Whitmore just as she was failing to save her very own mother. Her warnings had gone unheeded, her evidence dismissed as childish jealousy.

She followed the doctor to his next appointment, gathering her courage as she approached him outside his patient's house.

"Excuse me, sir," she called, adopting her most polite tone. "Might I ask about Mrs. Whitmore's condition? I'm from St. Michael's Church, and we've been most concerned."

The doctor, a grey-haired man with kind eyes, looked down at her with professional gravity. "I'm sorry to inform you that Mrs. Whitmore passed away this morning. A most puzzling case with symptoms suggesting gastric inflammation but progressing far more rapidly than typical. Most unfortunate."

"Was anyone with her when she died?" Elizabeth asked.

"A young lady friend, Miss Ashworth, I believe. Most devoted. She'd been preparing herbal remedies to ease the poor woman's suffering." He sighed heavily. "Not that anything could have helped by the end. The human body sometimes fails in ways medical science cannot yet explain."

Or in ways medical science fails to recognise as deliberate poisoning, Elizabeth thought bitterly.

"Thank you, doctor. We'll remember Mrs. Whitmore in our prayers."

She turned away, blinking back tears of frustration. Another death. Another murder disguised as a natural illness. And soon her mother would join the growing list of Veronica's victims.

As if summoned by this thought, Elizabeth spotted a familiar figure across the street. Veronica herself, dressed in appropriate mourning attire, was emerging from Mrs. Whitmore's house. Instead of showing grief for her "dear friend," Veronica's face bore an expression of calm satisfaction as she consulted a small notebook before tucking it into her reticule.

Elizabeth ducked behind a carriage to avoid being seen. From her hiding place, she watched Veronica speak briefly with a man who appeared to be a solicitor, nodding as he showed her some documents. Even at a distance, Elizabeth could read the triumph in her posture.

The business concluded, Veronica walked briskly toward the main road, her step light despite her sombre clothing. Elizabeth followed at a safe distance, trailing her through London's busy streets until she reached a familiar destination: the offices of Flanders Imports.

Through the window, Elizabeth watched as Veronica entered her father's private office. William rose to greet her, his face lighting up with pleasure at her unexpected visit. She spoke animatedly, showing him some paper, likely documentation of Mrs. Whitmore's death or perhaps her will. Whatever the news, it clearly delighted William. He embraced Veronica with obvious affection, lifting her off her feet in his enthusiasm.

The display of celebration over a woman's death, a death Veronica had methodically orchestrated, made bile rise in Elizabeth's throat. Her father was not merely bewitched; he was complicit, whether through wilful blindness or active participation.

She turned away, unable to bear the sight any longer. As she walked slowly home, the pieces fell into terrible alignment in her mind. Veronica had established a perfect system: identify wealthy, isolated women; befriend them; ensure they altered their wills in her favour; poison them slowly to avoid suspicion; collect the inheritance; and move to the next victim.

And William, what was his role? Did he know the truth and choose to ignore it because Veronica's blood money benefited his own criminal enterprise? Or was he genuinely blind to her methods, accepting her sudden "inheritances" from "distant relatives" and "dear friends" without question?

Either possibility painted her father in a damning light. The man who had once justified grave robbing as serving medical science now profited from actual murder, either knowingly or through deliberate ignorance.

Elizabeth reached their home and paused at the front steps, suddenly reluctant to enter. This was no longer the house of her childhood, with its veneer of respectability covering her father's nocturnal activities. It had become something far darker: a place where murder was planned, where her mother lay dying by inches, where Elizabeth herself might soon join the list of inconvenient persons eliminated for profit.

Yet where else could she go? A twelve-year-old girl alone in London would face dangers perhaps even greater than those within these familiar walls. For now, she must return, must watch, must gather evidence that even her father couldn't dismiss.

Because if she failed, Mary Flanders would not be Veronica's final victim in this house. And Elizabeth had no intention of becoming an entry in that meticulous notebook of the dead.

CHAPTER 5

Elizabeth stood in the church vestry, her black mourning dress a silent protest among the handful of wedding guests. Outside, a cold March rain lashed against the windows, as if nature itself objected to the ceremony taking place a mere six weeks after her mother's death. The hasty marriage violated every social convention of proper mourning, but William Flanders had never been a man to bow to society's expectations, especially now, with respectable society having long since turned its back on the family.

"Straighten your collar," Veronica instructed, adjusting her own wedding ensemble, a dress of pale lavender that deliberately avoided both bridal white and mourning black. "You look like a scarecrow."

Elizabeth obeyed mechanically, her fingers fumbling with the stiff fabric. At thirteen, she was too old to weep openly for her mother, and too young to refuse her father's demand that she serve as Veronica's bridesmaid. The role felt like a final betrayal of Mary Flanders, whose body had barely cooled in its grave before her husband sought to replace her.

"There now," Veronica continued, studying herself in the small mirror. "Not the wedding I might have hoped for, but it serves its purpose." Her violet eyes met Elizabeth's in the reflection. "Don't look so tragic, child. One might think you're not happy for your father's new chance at love."

The mockery in her tone made Elizabeth's stomach clench. They both knew there was no love in this union, only Veronica's cold calculation and William's blind infatuation.

The church door opened, admitting Morris, one of William's grave-robbing associates. "Vicar says they're ready for you now, miss."

"Mrs. Flanders," Veronica corrected, testing her new title with evident satisfaction. "Come along, Elizabeth. Let's not keep your father waiting."

The ceremony itself was mercifully brief. No

family attended. Veronica claimed to be an orphan, though Elizabeth suspected this was yet another lie, and the only witnesses were men from William's criminal network. The vicar, a nervous man with darting eyes who had accepted a substantial payment to overlook the impropriety of the timing, rushed through the service as if expecting the authorities to interrupt at any moment.

Elizabeth watched her father place a gold band on Veronica's slender finger, his face alight with an adoration that had never been visible in his interactions with Mary. When he kissed his new bride, Elizabeth looked away, unable to bear the sight of his complete capitulation to the woman who had murdered her mother.

"Well, my daughter," William said afterwards, his arm possessively around Veronica's waist, "aren't you going to congratulate us?"

Elizabeth forced her lips into what she hoped resembled a smile. "Congratulations, Father." She turned to Veronica, the words like ash in her mouth. "And to you... Mother."

Veronica's laugh tinkled like breaking glass. "Oh no, my dear. 'Mother' won't do at all. I'm hardly old enough for such a matronly title." She stroked

William's cheek possessively. "You shall call me Veronica. After all, we're practically sisters, aren't we?"

The comparison, linking her to her mother's murderer, sent bile rising in Elizabeth's throat. But she swallowed it down, as she had swallowed so many bitter truths in recent years.

"As you wish," she murmured, knowing that the battle for her father's soul was already lost. Now she fought only for her own survival.

* * *

"TAKE these to the church donation box," Veronica ordered, gesturing to the trunks containing Mary's clothing. "The poor can make use of them."

Elizabeth stared at the three large trunks that held her mother's possessions: dresses she had once admired, shawls that still carried the faint scent of Mary's lavender water, gloves, bonnets, and all the accoutrements of a respectable woman's wardrobe.

"Might I keep something to remember her by?" she asked quietly.

Veronica's expression hardened. "Sentimentality is a weakness, Elizabeth. Your mother is gone. Her possessions are merely objects taking up valuable space." She turned to the new housemaid, a hard-faced woman who had replaced their longtime servant within days of the wedding. "Jenkins, see that these are removed immediately."

"Yes, ma'am." The maid began dragging the trunks toward the door.

Elizabeth watched helplessly as her mother's life was systematically erased from the house. Already, the changes were everywhere: Mary's portrait removed from the parlour wall, her books donated to a church sale, her sewing box emptied and repurposed for Veronica's jewellery. Even the blue Chinese vase Mary had loved now held flowers arranged to Veronica's taste, stark white lilies with their overpowering scent that reminded Elizabeth of funerals.

The transformation extended beyond physical objects. New servants loyal to Veronica replaced the staff who had known and respected Mary. The weekly charitable ladies' meetings Mary had hosted were cancelled, the household accounts transferred to Veronica's control, and even the menu changed to reflect the new mistress's preferences.

"The past is dead," William had declared when Elizabeth questioned these rapid changes. "Veronica brings fresh energy to our home. Embrace the future, my dear."

But the future Veronica created felt increasingly hostile to Elizabeth's presence. Her bedroom, once a sanctuary, was now regularly "inspected" for cleanliness, her possessions rearranged or removed without permission, her privacy violated under the guise of proper household management.

One morning, Elizabeth returned from school to find her room transformed, her books removed, her desk relocated to a dark corner, and her bed replaced with a narrower, less comfortable one.

"Your old bed has been moved to the guest room," Veronica explained when questioned. "This one is more appropriate for a girl your age. Too much comfort breeds laziness."

Elizabeth said nothing, recognising the petty tyranny for what it was: a demonstration of Veronica's absolute control over her environment. That night, she slipped her hand beneath the thin mattress and retrieved the one possession she had managed to hide, a small locket containing a strand of her mother's hair, secreted away before Veronica could dispose of all such mementoes.

The locket represented more than remembrance; it was evidence. For while the doctors had attributed

Mary's death to a wasting illness, Elizabeth had clipped this hair during her mother's final days, intending someday to have it tested for the poisons she knew Veronica had administered. It was a small act of defiance, but it kept alive her hope that justice might eventually be served.

* * *

THE HOUSE SETTLED into an uneasy rhythm under Veronica's rule. William, increasingly occupied with expanding his grave-robbing enterprise, spent less time at home, leaving Elizabeth alone with her stepmother for long stretches. These periods became exercises in vigilance, watching what she ate, listening for footsteps outside her door at night, and carefully maintaining a facade of submission while secretly observing Veronica's activities.

Three weeks after the wedding, Elizabeth seized an opportunity when Veronica departed for a "charitable visit" to another wealthy widow. She slipped into what had once been her mother's sitting room, now converted to Veronica's private study.

The room had been transformed like the rest of the house, with Mary's delicate writing desk replaced by a larger, more masculine piece, her watercolours exchanged for darker landscapes, her comfortable chairs removed in favour of a single imposing seat behind the desk. Even the wallpaper had been changed, and the soft floral pattern was covered with a striped design in blood-red and black.

Elizabeth moved quickly to the desk, trying the drawers that proved to be locked. She had anticipated this and came prepared with a thin wire she had bent for the purpose. Her father's criminal activities had provided an unconventional education, including lockpicking skills learned from observing his associates.

The centre drawer yielded first, revealing neat stacks of household accounts and correspondence; nothing incriminating but evidence of Veronica's methodical mind. The side drawers contained similar mundane items until Elizabeth noticed something odd about the right drawer, which seemed shallower inside than its exterior dimensions suggested.

Careful exploration revealed a false bottom, which lifted to expose a hidden compartment. Inside lay several folders, each labelled with a name Elizabeth recognised from her father's criminal network.

She opened the first labelled Morris, Thomas to

find detailed notes on the man's history, habits, family connections, and vulnerabilities. Veronica had documented his weakness for gin, his crippling gambling debts, and most damning, his involvement in a murder during a grave robbery gone wrong. Similar files existed for each of William's key associates, containing information that could send them to the gallows if revealed to authorities.

But the most disturbing file bore her father's name. Pages of observations detailed William's business methods, criminal connections, and most private habits. Notes in Veronica's elegant handwriting analysed his psychology: "Responds well to flattery regarding his intelligence. Becomes pliant when physical affection is withheld, then granted as a reward for compliance. Blind spot regarding daughter: views her as extension of self rather than independent threat."

The final page contained a list of William's assets, including bank accounts Elizabeth had never known existed and property holdings beyond their London home. Beside each item, Veronica had noted legal ownership status and what would be required to transfer control to herself in case of William's "incapacitation or demise."

Elizabeth's hands shook as she replaced the files

exactly as she had found them. This was not merely the record-keeping of a new wife; it was the strategic planning of someone who had targeted William from the beginning, positioning herself to either control or eliminate him when his usefulness ended.

She had just closed the drawer when a floorboard creaked in the hallway. Elizabeth froze, then forced herself to move naturally to the bookshelf as if merely looking for reading material. The door opened to reveal Veronica, returned earlier than expected, her eyes narrowing as she took in Elizabeth's presence in her private domain.

"Looking for something?" Veronica asked, her voice deceptively light.

"Just a book," Elizabeth replied, pulling a random volume from the shelf. "Father suggested I read more history."

"How studious of you." Veronica moved to her desk, glancing at the drawers with an assessing eye. "Though I don't recall giving you permission to enter my study."

"I apologise. I didn't realise it required permission." Elizabeth edged toward the door, clutching the book as a shield. "I won't disturb you further."

Veronica's hand shot out, grasping Elizabeth's

wrist with surprising strength. "Let me see what you've chosen."

She examined the book, a dry treatise on Roman architecture, before releasing Elizabeth with a small push. "Next time, ask before entering my private rooms. This house has rules now, Elizabeth. Breaking them has consequences."

The threat lingered in the air as Elizabeth retreated, her pulse racing with the knowledge that she had narrowly escaped discovery. Veronica suspected something; perhaps not the specific invasion of her files, but a general insubordination that she clearly would not tolerate.

From that day forward, Elizabeth noticed Veronica watching her more closely, assigning more household tasks to keep her occupied, and limiting her freedom to move about the house. The pretence of familial affection dropped away entirely when William was absent, replaced by the cold authority of a jailer monitoring a prisoner.

* * *

THE FIRST BEATING occurred a week later, triggered by what Veronica termed "impertinence" when Elizabeth questioned the dismissal of their cook, Mrs.

Perkins, the last servant remaining from her mother's time.

"Remove your dress," Veronica ordered, locking the door of the upstairs sewing room where she had cornered Elizabeth after dinner.

"I beg your pardon?" Elizabeth stared in confusion.

"Your dress. Remove it. I won't risk marking the fabric."

Understanding dawned with sickening clarity. "Father wouldn't allow this," Elizabeth said, backing toward the window.

Veronica laughed, retrieving a riding crop from behind a sewing basket. "Your father authorised me to discipline you as I see fit. His exact words were, 'The girl needs a firmer hand than I've provided.' He's currently meeting with associates in Whitechapel and won't return until morning. We have ample time for your lesson."

Elizabeth considered screaming, but the new servants were all Veronica's creatures, unlikely to intervene. The window offered no escape from the second floor. She was trapped.

"Now, Elizabeth. Or I'll add disobedience to your offences."

With trembling fingers, Elizabeth unfastened her

dress, allowing it to pool at her feet. Standing in her thin chemise and petticoats, she felt exposed and vulnerable, exactly as Veronica intended.

"Turn around. Hands on the wall."

The first strike caught Elizabeth between her shoulder blades, the pain shocking in its intensity. The second landed lower, the third lower still, each precise blow calculated to cause maximum pain without leaving visible marks that might raise William's concern.

"This is your position now," Veronica explained between strikes, her voice calm and instructional. "You exist in this house on my sufferance. You will obey me without question. You will maintain a respectful demeanour at all times." Another blow emphasised each point. "You will never again interfere with my household decisions or question my authority."

Elizabeth bit her lip until she tasted blood, refusing to give Veronica the satisfaction of hearing her cry out. Each stroke burned like fire across her back, but worse than the physical pain was the humiliation of being treated like an animal, punished at the whim of the woman who had murdered her mother and now controlled her father.

When it finally ended, Veronica stepped back, breathing slightly faster but otherwise showing no emotion. "Get dressed. Your face is flushed, and go directly to your room. If your father asks, tell him you're feeling unwell."

Elizabeth pulled her dress on with shaking hands, each movement sending fresh pain through her abused back. As she fastened the buttons, Veronica caught her chin, forcing their eyes to meet.

"This is merely a taste of what awaits if you continue to resist me," she said softly. "I can make your life bearable or unbearable; the choice is yours. Remember that the next time you consider defying me."

That night, lying face-down on her bed, Elizabeth wept silently into her pillow. Not from the pain, though it throbbed with every heartbeat, but from the realisation of how completely trapped she had become. Her father, once her protector despite his criminal activities, had abdicated that role, handing her over to a woman who enjoyed inflicting suffering.

She had no allies in the household, no friends outside it since their social disgrace, and nowhere to flee even if escape were possible. At thirteen, alone in London without resources, she would face dangers perhaps even worse than Veronica's calculated cruelty.

For now, survival meant submission, or at least the appearance of it. But as Elizabeth drifted into uneasy sleep, she promised herself that this submission was temporary. She would watch, wait, and learn, gathering knowledge as armour against the day when she might finally break free.

* * *

OVER THE FOLLOWING WEEKS, Elizabeth maintained a careful facade of obedience while secretly documenting Veronica's activities. She observed her stepmother's continuing pattern of targeting wealthy widows, noting names and addresses in a small notebook hidden beneath a loose floorboard in her bedroom.

The routine was always the same: Veronica would identify a potential victim, establish contact through church or charitable work, cultivate a friendship over several weeks, then begin administering her "special remedies" when the victim complained of minor ailments. The poisoning would progress gradually, with doctors baffled by symptoms that mimicked natural disease. By the time death occurred, Veronica had usually secured a place in the victim's will or positioned herself to acquire valuable possessions during the subsequent confusion.

Elizabeth's most disturbing discovery came when she managed to access Veronica's private record book during one of her stepmother's absences. Hidden in a locked cabinet in the conservatory, the leather-bound volume contained detailed accounts of at least twelve women who had died under Veronica's care over the past three years. Each entry included the victim's financial status, the poison used, the timeline of administration, and the profits secured.

The most recent entry chilled Elizabeth's blood:

Mrs. Eleanor Ashford, 62. Widow of banking fortune. No living children. Foxglove primary agent, supplemented with small amounts of arsenic. Duration: 24 days from initial dose to expiration. Assets acquired: £3,200 in cash bequest, jewellery valued at approximately £800, small property in Kent (potential income £120 annually). Excellent result with minimal complication.

The clinical detachment with which Veronica documented her murders revealed a mind devoid of conscience or remorse. These weren't crimes of passion or desperation, but a systematic business enterprise built on suffering and death.

Elizabeth carefully replaced the book, her mind racing with the implications of her discovery. The evidence she now possessed could send Veronica to the gallows, if only someone would believe the accusations of a thirteen-year-old girl against a respectable married woman.

Her father was beyond reach, his infatuation with Veronica having hardened into dependence. The authorities would dismiss her without proof she could physically produce. And approaching Veronica's intended victims carried its own risks; they might report her warnings to Veronica herself, hastening Elizabeth's own danger.

For now, knowledge was her only weapon; knowledge and vigilance against the day when Veronica inevitably turned her poisoner's skills against the last remaining obstacle to her complete control of the Flanders household and fortune.

That day came sooner than Elizabeth expected. Returning early from school due to a teacher's illness, she overheard voices from her father's study belonging to Veronica and William in what appeared to be a serious discussion. She paused outside the partially open door, listening.

"—concerning symptoms," Veronica was saying, her voice carrying the professional concern she typically used when discussing her victims' health. "Loss of appetite, occasional dizziness, pallor. Dr. Morrison should examine her."

"Elizabeth has always been robust," William replied, sounding genuinely worried. "Perhaps it's merely the strain of adjusting to our new family arrangement."

"Perhaps. But these symptoms appeared suddenly, and given her age, we must be vigilant. Young girls can develop consumption or nervous conditions with alarming rapidity."

Elizabeth's blood ran cold. She had exhibited none of the symptoms Veronica described; this was the opening gambit in her stepmother's familiar strategy. First, plant the idea of illness in the minds of those surrounding the victim. Next, introduce "helpful" remedies that actually cause the symptoms previously described. Finally, escalate the poisoning as doctors fail to identify the true cause of deteriorating health.

"I've prepared a tonic that might help," Veronica continued. "A family recipe particularly effective for girls entering womanhood. My grandmother swore by it."

"You're always so thoughtful," William said, his voice warming with affection. "What would I do without you to manage these domestic matters?"

"You'll never need to find out," Veronica assured him. "Now, about expanding our operations to the new cemetery in Nunhead, I've identified several potential informants among the groundskeepers."

Elizabeth backed away from the door, her heart pounding. The conversation had shifted to business matters, but the damage was done. Veronica had begun laying the groundwork for her murder, and William had accepted the premise without question.

That evening at dinner, Veronica presented Elizabeth with a small glass of dark liquid.

"A tonic to restore your strength," she explained, her violet eyes watching carefully for any sign of resistance. "Your father and I are concerned about your health."

Elizabeth knew refusal would provoke immediate suspicion. "How thoughtful," she said, raising the glass to her lips but not drinking. "Though I feel perfectly well."

"Preventative care is essential for growing girls," Veronica insisted. "Drink it all, dear. It's quite effective, though admittedly not pleasant tasting."

William nodded encouragingly from across the

table. "Do as Veronica suggests, Elizabeth. She has your best interests at heart."

With no option for outright refusal, Elizabeth pretended to sip while actually allowing the liquid to wet only her lips. The bitter taste confirmed her suspicions that this was no innocent tonic but the beginning of her systematic poisoning.

"I'll take the remainder to my room," she said, standing with the glass still mostly full. "The taste is rather strong. Perhaps drinking it before bed would be easier."

Veronica's eyes narrowed slightly. "As you wish. But do finish it, Elizabeth. Your health depends on regular treatment."

In her room, Elizabeth poured the "tonic" into a jar she had hidden for this purpose, sealing it carefully for future evidence. She had anticipated this moment, knowing that Veronica would eventually tire of more subtle torments and move to eliminate her permanently.

The danger had now become immediate. Each meal, each drink, each sweet or medicine offered might contain poison. Elizabeth began implementing the survival strategies she had developed during her weeks of observation: eating only food she had seen others consume, drinking water she poured herself, and maintaining the appearance of deteriorating health to satisfy Veronica's expectations.

She feigned occasional dizziness, picked at her meals, claiming loss of appetite, and allowed her complexion to appear paler through subtle adjustments to her washing routine. The deception bought time, but Elizabeth harboured no illusions about its sustainability. Veronica would expect increasingly serious symptoms, and when they didn't materialise naturally, she would escalate her poisoning attempts.

One night, unable to sleep for worry, Elizabeth crept downstairs to retrieve a book from the parlour. Passing her father's study, she heard voices despite the late hour. William and Veronica were reviewing business matters, their tones animated with plans and ambitions.

"The Highgate operation alone brought twenty pounds last week," William was saying. "With the new contacts at Guy's Hospital, we could double that figure."

"Excellent," Veronica replied. "And with the proceeds from the Ashford bequest, we can expand further. I've identified three more promising cemetery locations."

"Your business acumen continues to impress me,

my dear. I never imagined a woman could have such a head for these matters."

"Women are often underestimated," Veronica said, a smile evident in her voice. "Speaking of which, have you noticed any improvement in Elizabeth's condition?"

A pause. "She does seem paler, more subdued. Your tonic appears to be having some effect."

"The initial stages are subtle. But don't worry, I'll monitor her closely. These conditions can progress quite rapidly in the young. Sometimes a decline that seems gradual suddenly accelerates."

"Poor child," William murmured, though without great emotion. "First her mother, now her own health. Life can be cruel."

"Indeed. But we must be practical. Should the worst occur, her portion of the business would revert to you as her father, would it not?"

"Naturally. Although I've never formally documented her share. It seemed unnecessary given her age."

"Still, perhaps we should consult a solicitor. Just to ensure everything is properly arranged. For Elizabeth's security, of course."

Elizabeth pressed her hand against her mouth to stifle a gasp. Veronica wasn't merely planning her death, she was ensuring the financial arrangements would benefit herself through William. And her father, rather than protecting his daughter, was discussing her potential demise with the detached interest of a businessman reviewing an underperforming asset.

She retreated silently to her room, the reality of her situation crystallising with terrible clarity. Her father had become a willing tool in Veronica's hands, blind to the manipulation that had transformed him from a criminal with certain moral boundaries into an accomplice to premeditated murder; the murder of his own child.

Elizabeth sat on her narrow bed, moonlight casting harsh shadows across the floor as she considered her options. She could no longer pretend that survival within this house was possible. Veronica's patience would eventually wear thin, and a more direct method of elimination would replace the gradual poisoning. A "tragic accident", perhaps, or a sudden "fever" that carried her off before medical help could arrive.

The time for watching and waiting had ended. If Elizabeth remained, she would join her mother and Mrs. Whitmore and Mrs. Ashford and all the other women whose lives had been methodically extinguished for profit. Her only hope lay in escape, immediate and complete, leaving behind everything she had known for the uncertain dangers of London's streets.

As she began mentally cataloguing what few possessions she might take, Elizabeth acknowledged the bitter truth that had been building since her mother's death. The respectable life she had once known, with its veneer of propriety covering darker secrets, had shattered completely. Her father's moral compromise had progressed to the point where he would sacrifice his own daughter for the approval of a beautiful, manipulative murderer.

Elizabeth had become the final inconvenient obstacle to Veronica's complete triumph, the last witness to her crimes, the last connection to William's previous life, the last person who might someday expose the truth. And in Veronica's methodical world, obstacles existed to be eliminated.

The choice now was stark: submit completely to a slow death by poisoning or flee into London's dangerous streets with nothing but her wits to protect her. Neither option promised safety or comfort, but only one offered the possibility of survival.

Elizabeth made her decision as the moon disappeared behind clouds, plunging her room into darkness that matched the future before her. She would gather what she could, wait for the right moment, and vanish from the house that had transformed from a haven to a death trap under Veronica's malevolent influence.

Whether she would survive what came after, only time would tell.

CHAPTER 6

Elizabeth pressed her ear against the study door, straining to catch the murmured conversation within. Veronica's voice, usually so controlled, carried an unfamiliar note of urgency.

"The operation at Kensal Green yielded three bodies last month without incident," she was saying to someone Elizabeth couldn't identify. "My husband's network extends to five major cemeteries, with regular deliveries to St. Bartholomew's, Guy's Hospital, and the Royal College."

A man's voice responded, too low for Elizabeth to distinguish the words.

"Yes, Inspector Harrison. I can provide names, dates, and locations of planned excavations." A pause. "I understand the gravity of turning informant against my own husband, but my conscience can bear this burden no longer."

Elizabeth's breath caught. Inspector Harrison of the Metropolitan Police. And Veronica was providing information about William's grave robbing business, posing as a reluctant informant driven by moral qualms.

The irony might have been laughable if the implications weren't so deadly serious. Veronica, who had poisoned at least a dozen women, who had murdered Elizabeth's mother, who had beaten Elizabeth herself with calculated cruelty, suddenly developing a conscience?

No. This was something else entirely.

Elizabeth retreated silently as footsteps approached the door. She slipped into the adjacent parlour just as the study opened, revealing Veronica escorting a plain-clothed man to the front entrance. Though dressed as a tradesman, his bearing suggested authority. Inspector Harrison disguised himself for this clandestine meeting.

"I'll send word when I have the details of Wednesday's operation," Veronica said, her voice carrying just enough distress to sound convincing.

"Please remember your promise of discretion. If William suspected I'd spoken to the police..."

"Your safety is assured, Mrs. Flanders," the inspector replied. "Your cooperation will be noted favourably should questions arise about your own involvement."

After he departed, Veronica remained in the hallway for a moment. When she turned toward the parlour, Elizabeth glimpsed something that chilled her blood; not the mask of distress Veronica had shown the inspector, but a smile of pure satisfaction.

The pieces aligned in Elizabeth's mind with terrible clarity. Veronica wasn't acting out of a sudden moral awakening or fear of criminal association. She was orchestrating William's downfall with the same methodical precision she had applied to poisoning her victims.

But why? William was already under her control, his criminal profits funding their comfortable lifestyle, his devotion to her complete.

The answer came as Elizabeth recalled the files she had discovered: Veronica's detailed accounting of William's assets and what would be required to transfer them to herself. With William transported to Australia or imprisoned for life, Veronica would gain control of everything, free to continue her poisoning enterprise without his knowledge or interference.

Elizabeth had delayed her own escape too long, fascinated by this unfolding betrayal like a mouse watching a snake, unable to look away from the deadly dance. Now she could only observe as Veronica spun her web around the husband who trusted her absolutely, and wait for her own moment to flee before becoming the next victim.

* * *

"THE HIGHGATE OPERATION must proceed tomorrow night," Veronica insisted, leaning over the map spread across William's desk. "My sources confirm the Edwards burial occurred this morning; a perfect specimen for the Royal College."

William frowned, studying the cemetery layout. "Highgate has increased security since the Marlowe incident. Jenkins reported additional night watchmen patrolling the north section."

"Which is precisely why the Edwards plot is ideal: south quadrant, minimal surveillance, recently disturbed earth for easy excavation." Veronica traced the route with a slender finger. "A simple extraction, substantial profit."

Elizabeth, supposedly reading in the corner but actually absorbing every word, noted how Veronica's guidance consistently pushed her father toward greater risks. In the month since she had overheard the meeting with Inspector Harrison, Veronica had steered William's operations toward increasingly dangerous territories: well-guarded cemeteries, prominent families whose deaths attracted attention, and expanded operations during periods of increased police vigilance.

"Morris disagrees," William said, rubbing his chin thoughtfully. "He suggests waiting until next week when the moon is less full."

"Morris lacks vision," Veronica countered smoothly. "The medical schools won't pay premium rates for decomposed specimens. Timing is essential." She placed her hand over William's. "Trust me, husband. Have I ever steered you wrong?"

The question hung in the air, heavy with irony that only Elizabeth recognised. Of course, Veronica had never "steered him wrong" in business matters; her intelligence and strategic thinking had expanded his criminal enterprise substantially. That was the perfect cover for her betrayal; she had built his trust through genuine success before leveraging it for his destruction.

"Very well," William conceded, covering her hand with his own. "Tomorrow night. I'll inform the men."

From her corner, Elizabeth watched an almost imperceptible smile curve Veronica's lips, triumph carefully concealed beneath wifely devotion. The trap was set.

Later that evening, while William met with his grave-robbing team in his study, Elizabeth observed Veronica writing a note at her desk. When finished, she sealed it carefully and slipped out to the garden, where she handed the folded paper to a boy waiting by the gate. Coins changed hands, and the boy darted away into the gathering darkness.

Elizabeth didn't need to see the note's contents or know its destination to understand its purpose. Veronica had just provided Inspector Harrison with the exact details needed to catch William and his men in the act: date, time, location, and participants in tomorrow's planned grave robbery.

The betrayal was now inevitable. Elizabeth considered warning her father, but discarded the thought immediately. He wouldn't believe her over Veronica, and any interference would only accelerate Veronica's plans for Elizabeth herself.

Instead, she retreated to her room and continued preparations for her own escape. The small bundle hidden under her bed contained essential items collected over weeks: a change of clothing, her mother's locket, the few coins she had managed to save, and most precious, the evidence of Veronica's poisoning activities she had painstakingly gathered.

Tomorrow night, the attention focused on William's arrest might provide her opportunity to flee. Elizabeth lay awake planning routes through London, considering potential refuges, imagining survival strategies for a fourteen-year-old girl alone in the city's unforgiving streets.

The future held nothing but uncertainty, but one thing was clear: she could not remain in this house after William's removal. Without his presence, however morally compromised, there would be nothing to restrain Veronica's actions toward her inconvenient stepdaughter.

* * *

THE FOLLOWING NIGHT, Elizabeth watched from her bedroom window as William and three associates departed for Highgate Cemetery. The moon illuminated their figures as they moved through the garden gate, carrying the tools of their grim trade, shovels disguised in canvas wrappings, lanterns unlit until needed, and burlap sacks for transporting their macabre cargo.

Her father glanced back at the house before disappearing into the darkness, perhaps seeking a glimpse of Veronica watching his departure. But Veronica wasn't at her usual window. She was in her study, dressed not for bed but for potential visitors, her appearance immaculate despite the late hour.

Elizabeth considered implementing her escape plan immediately, but hesitated, drawn by morbid fascination with the drama unfolding. She wanted—needed—to witness Veronica's reaction when her betrayal bore fruit.

The house settled into uneasy silence. Servants had long since retired to their quarters, leaving the main rooms dark except for the faint light from Veronica's study. Elizabeth crept downstairs, positioning herself in the shadows of the hallway where she could observe without being seen.

The mantel clock had just struck one when a sharp knock came at the front door. Veronica emerged from her study instantly, smoothing her skirts before opening the door to admit Inspector Harrison, now in full uniform, accompanied by two constables.

"Mrs. Flanders," he said, removing his hat. "I

regret to inform you that we've apprehended your husband and his associates at Highgate Cemetery, engaged in the unlawful exhumation of a recently deceased person."

Veronica's performance was flawless: a gasp of shock, a hand pressed to her heart, her body swaying slightly as if overcome. "There must be some mistake," she whispered.

"I'm afraid not, ma'am. They were caught in the act, with evidence that cannot be disputed." Harrison's tone softened slightly. "Your information proved entirely accurate. The Crown appreciates your courage in coming forward."

"My information?" Veronica's voice rose in perfect simulation of distress. "I don't understand."

"Come now, Mrs. Flanders. There's no need for pretence among ourselves." Harrison glanced at his constables. "Your written statement regarding your husband's criminal activities will be treated with appropriate discretion, as agreed."

"I made no statement!" Veronica protested, tears now flowing down her cheeks. "I would never betray my husband!"

Elizabeth watched in reluctant admiration as Veronica maintained her innocence, playing the role of shocked wife so convincingly that even Harrison seemed momentarily uncertain.

"Perhaps we should continue this discussion at the station," he suggested. "Your presence will be required to complete the necessary documentation."

"Of course," Veronica murmured, reaching for her shawl. "Though I still cannot fathom how this terrible mistake occurred."

As the inspector escorted Veronica out, Elizabeth caught a final glimpse of her stepmother's face. The mask of distress slipped for just an instant, revealing cold satisfaction beneath, a predator who had successfully cornered her prey.

Elizabeth waited until the police carriage departed before racing to her room to retrieve her escape bundle. With both William and Veronica away, this was her perfect opportunity to flee.

Yet, as she reached for the bundle beneath her bed, a new thought stopped her. Veronica would return before William, who would likely remain in custody until his hearing. If Elizabeth disappeared tonight, Veronica would immediately suspect she had witnessed the betrayal. She would alert authorities, perhaps claiming Elizabeth had been involved in her father's crimes, making her a fugitive from justice as well as a runaway.

Better to wait, to maintain the pretence of ignorance, to observe Veronica's next moves before acting. Elizabeth reluctantly pushed the bundle deeper under the bed. Her escape would have to wait for a more strategic moment.

From her window, she could see Highgate Cemetery in the distance, imagining her father's shock as police surrounded him, the sudden realisation of betrayal as he was led away in handcuffs. Despite his crimes, despite his moral failings, Elizabeth felt a pang of sympathy for the man who had loved unwisely and trusted completely the woman who engineered his downfall.

* * *

William's trial became a public spectacle that drew curious onlookers and newspaper reporters eager for details of the "Respectable Merchant's Descent into Grave Robbery." Elizabeth sat in the crowded gallery, watching her father stand in the dock, his once-confident posture now diminished by weeks in Newgate Prison awaiting trial.

Beside her sat Veronica, dressed in sombre colours suggesting distress without the full mourning that might appear presumptuous. Her performance of the devastated wife continued flawlessly, dabbing at tears with a lace handkerchief, leaning on Elizabeth's shoulder for support, whispering prayers for mercy that carried just far enough for nearby spectators to overhear.

The evidence against William was overwhelming. Police testimony described finding him and his associates with a partially exhumed coffin, specialised tools for quick and quiet grave opening, and a history of similar activities documented through informant statements and financial records seized from his office.

William maintained a stoic expression throughout most of the proceedings, speaking only to confirm his name and enter his plea of guilty, a strategic choice his solicitor had advised might result in a reduced sentence. His gaze frequently sought Veronica in the gallery, drawing strength from her apparent devotion, completely blind to her betrayal.

Then came the moment Elizabeth had dreaded: Veronica's testimony.

"Mrs. Flanders," the prosecutor began once she was sworn in, "when did you become aware of your husband's criminal activities?"

Veronica's voice trembled appropriately. "Only

recently, sir. I discovered financial records that couldn't be explained by his import business. When confronted, my husband admitted the truth."

"And what was your reaction to this discovery?"

"Horror, sir. Absolute horror." Her violet eyes filled with perfectly timed tears. "I begged him to stop, to consider the moral implications, but he refused."

"Did you take any action upon learning this information?"

A hesitation, as if reluctant to answer. "I... I felt I had no choice but to inform the authorities. The desecration of graves is an offence against both law and God."

Elizabeth dug her nails into her palms, fighting the urge to stand and denounce the hypocrisy. Veronica, who had murdered multiple women for profit, who had poisoned Elizabeth's mother, who had beaten Elizabeth with calculated cruelty, was now positioning herself as the moral conscience of the family.

"That must have been a difficult decision, Mrs. Flanders," the prosecutor said sympathetically.

"The most difficult of my life," Veronica agreed, her voice breaking. "I love my husband deeply, but I could not be complicit in such acts."

William's expression crumbled at these words. For the first time, doubt clouded his eyes as he stared at his wife, not yet comprehending the full extent of her betrayal, but beginning to question the narrative she presented.

The judge's verdict surprised no one: transportation to Australia for fourteen years. As the sentence was pronounced, William looked toward Veronica one last time. Elizabeth couldn't read his expression clearly: confusion, betrayal, lingering love despite everything, but she recognised the moment when reality began to penetrate his blind devotion.

Veronica wept convincingly as William was led away, accepting condolences from court officials who praised her moral courage. Elizabeth remained silent beside her, maintaining the expected demeanour of a dutiful daughter while inwardly calculating how this development affected her own precarious position.

With William gone, Veronica would have complete control over the household, the finances, and Elizabeth herself. The pretence of family harmony would no longer be necessary, and whatever restraint Veronica had shown in her treatment of Elizabeth would likely vanish.

The time for escape was approaching rapidly.

Elizabeth just needed to maintain her facade of ignorant compliance a little longer, until Veronica's vigilance relaxed and opportunity presented itself.

* * *

THE CHANGE in Veronica once they returned home from the trial was immediate and chilling. The mask of the grieving wife slipped away like a discarded garment, replaced by the cold authority of a victor claiming spoils.

"Your father's study needs clearing," she announced, guiding Elizabeth into the room that had been William's domain. "Remove his personal items. Anything of business value remains."

"Where shall I put his things?" Elizabeth asked, maintaining her role as the obedient stepdaughter.

"The attic. Or the rubbish. It hardly matters." Veronica ran her fingers possessively over the mahogany desk. "He won't be returning to claim them."

The casual cruelty of the statement hung in the air between them. No longer was there any pretence that Veronica had informed on William reluctantly or that she anticipated his eventual return. His removal had been permanent by design, his transportation a victory to be savoured.

Over the following weeks, Elizabeth witnessed Veronica's complete transformation of the household. William's associates were dismissed, his legitimate import business sold, and his criminal network either dispersed or absorbed into new arrangements under Veronica's direction. She maintained certain profitable aspects of the grave robbing enterprise but operated with greater caution, using intermediaries rather than direct involvement.

Meanwhile, her treatment of Elizabeth deteriorated from casual cruelty to systematic abuse. Meals became irregular and insufficient, household tasks multiplied beyond reasonable expectations, and physical punishment occurred with increasing frequency for infractions both real and imagined.

"You exist by my tolerance alone," Veronica explained during one such punishment, applying her riding crop with methodical precision to Elizabeth's back. "Your father abandoned you to my care, and I find you increasingly burdensome."

Elizabeth endured in silence, showing neither defiance nor submission. Each blow strengthened her resolve to escape, each humiliation another reason to persevere until opportunity arose. She documented her mistreatment in a hidden journal, recording dates, injuries, and witnesses; evidence she had little hope of using but maintained nonetheless, clinging to the possibility of eventual justice.

The household staff, already reduced after William's arrest, dwindled further as Veronica dismissed anyone showing kindness to Elizabeth. New servants arrived, hard-faced women and sullen men who turned blind eyes to Elizabeth's mistreatment or actively participated in her torment.

Veronica's behaviour grew increasingly erratic as weeks passed. Elizabeth observed her stepmother drinking heavily in the evenings, sometimes entertaining men who were neither business associates nor social acquaintances but something more intimate. These visitors never acknowledged Elizabeth's presence, treating her as invisible when they encountered her in hallways or on stairs.

The final catalyst came on a cold October night, nearly three months after William's transportation. Elizabeth, finishing late kitchen duties, heard Veronica call for her from the study. William's former study, now transformed with feminine touches that somehow made it more rather than less forbidding.

She found her stepmother slouched in the leather

chair behind the desk, a crystal decanter of brandy half-empty beside her. Veronica's usually immaculate appearance had deteriorated with her hair loosened from its pins, cheeks flushed with alcohol, and eyes bright with dangerous energy.

"You wanted me, Mrs. Flanders?" Elizabeth asked, using the formal address Veronica preferred.

"Mrs. Flanders," Veronica repeated, her voice slurred but still carrying its customary edge. "Such a respectable title for a woman who arranged her husband's transportation and her predecessor's death." She laughed, pouring more brandy with unsteady hands. "Come closer, girl. I dislike speaking to shadows."

Elizabeth approached cautiously, stopping just beyond arm's reach. Veronica, in this state, was unpredictable: sometimes maudlin, sometimes vicious.

"Do you know why I kept you this long?" Veronica asked, studying Elizabeth through narrowed eyes. "Convenience. A respectable household needs a daughter. Appearances matter." She took another swallow of brandy. "But you've outlived your usefulness. Watching, always watching with those accusing eyes. Just like your mother."

"I've completed my chores," Elizabeth said neutrally. "If there's nothing else—"

"There is something else." Veronica stood suddenly, moving with the deliberate care of the deeply intoxicated. "There's the matter of your future. Or rather, your lack of one."

She circled the desk, brandy glass dangling from her fingers. "Your father was a fool. Talented in his way, organised, methodical, but blind where pretty faces were concerned." A contemptuous smile curved her lips. "So easy to manipulate. A touch here, a compliment there, and he handed me everything: his business, his home, his daughter."

"You betrayed him," Elizabeth said quietly, abandoning pretence. "You informed on him to the police."

"Of course I did." Veronica seemed amused rather than concerned by Elizabeth's knowledge. "Transportation was cleaner than poison, less suspicious for a healthy man in his prime. And it left me in control of all assets without tedious legal complications."

She moved closer, alcohol fumes surrounding her like a noxious cloud. "I've been eliminating obstacles my entire life, Elizabeth. Your mother was merely one of many. Old women, sick women, inconvenient women all removed with appropriate discretion."

"You're a murderer," Elizabeth stated flatly.

"I'm a businesswoman," Veronica corrected, her tone almost professorial despite her intoxication. "Death is my business. Whether selling corpses your father exhumed or creating fresh ones through my own methods, it's all inventory management."

She drained her glass and set it down with exaggerated care. "But you. You've been my most challenging project. The watchful child who sees too much. The living reminder of that insipid woman I replaced. The potential witness to activities best left undocumented."

The threat hung in the air between them, no longer veiled by pretence or social niceties. Elizabeth tensed, ready to flee if Veronica moved toward her.

"I've been patient," Veronica continued, her voice hardening. "Poisoning is my preferred method—clean, controllable, difficult to detect. But you've been clever, haven't you? Avoiding my special teas, checking your food, watching for tampering." She laughed suddenly, the sound chilling in its genuine amusement. "I almost admire your survival instinct.

But patience has limits, and mine has reached its end."

Veronica moved to a cabinet, withdrawing something that glinted in the lamplight: a small pistol, its metal surface reflecting the room in distorted miniature.

"Your father kept this for protection. Ironic that it should serve to eliminate his precious daughter." She examined the weapon with casual interest. "A tragic accident while cleaning a firearm, not realising it was loaded. Such things happen in respectable households. Brief scandal, quickly forgotten."

Elizabeth took a step backwards, heart pounding against her ribs. "People will ask questions."

"What people? You have no friends, no allies. The servants are loyal to me. The neighbours avoid this house since your father's disgrace." Veronica raised the pistol, not quite pointing it at Elizabeth but making her intention clear. "No one will mourn you, Elizabeth. No one will even notice you're gone."

With shocking swiftness, Veronica lunged forward, her intoxication seemingly evaporating as she grabbed Elizabeth's arm with bruising force. "I've destroyed everyone who stood in my path: wealthy widows, your pathetic mother, your criminal father.

Did you really think a child would present any challenge?"

Elizabeth twisted free, desperation lending her strength. She backed toward the door, maintaining eye contact with Veronica as one might with a dangerous animal.

"You won't escape," Veronica said calmly, raising the pistol. "Accept your fate with dignity. It's more than your mother managed."

The mention of her mother sparked something in Elizabeth, not fear but cold rage. This woman had taken everything from her: family, home, safety, and future. She would not take her life as well.

With sudden decision, Elizabeth grabbed a heavy paperweight from a side table and hurled it at the lamp on the desk. Glass shattered, oil spilt, and flames erupted across papers and wood. Veronica screamed in surprise, momentarily distracted by the fire spreading across her precious records.

Elizabeth seized the opportunity, bolting from the room and up the stairs to her bedroom. She dragged her escape bundle from beneath the bed, hands shaking with urgency. From below came crashes and curses as Veronica presumably fought the fire.

There was no time for hesitation or second

thoughts. Elizabeth shoved her few possessions into a small satchel, pulled on her warmest coat, and slipped out her bedroom window onto the sloped roof of the kitchen extension. She had practised this route in her mind dozens of times: across the roof, down the trellis, through the garden to the rear gate that opened into an alley.

The night air bit through her thin clothing as she scrambled across the tiles, her breath forming white clouds in the October chill. Behind her, shouts indicated the household had been roused by the fire. Whether Veronica would pursue her immediately or deal with the blaze first remained uncertain.

Elizabeth dropped the last few feet from the trellis to the ground, pain shooting through her ankles at the impact. She stumbled but kept moving, racing through the moonlit garden toward the gate that represented her first step toward freedom.

The iron latch lifted easily, and then she was through, running down the narrow alley that connected to the street beyond. Fog had rolled in from the Thames, shrouding the neighbourhood in ghostly white that concealed her flight while simultaneously disorienting her planned route.

She paused at the alley's end, listening for pursuit. Hearing nothing but distant shouts related to the fire, Elizabeth pulled her coat tighter and plunged into the fog-shrouded streets of London.

She had no destination, no plan beyond immediate escape, and no understanding of how to survive on the streets. Her entire life had been spent in a household that, however morally corrupt, had provided shelter, food, and the structure of respectability. Now she faced a world where none of those certainties existed.

The gravity of her situation pressed down as she hurried through unfamiliar streets, trying to put maximum distance between herself and the house where Veronica waited with murder in her heart. Elizabeth had escaped immediate death, but survival remained far from guaranteed.

London at night was no place for a solitary girl of fourteen. Shadowy figures moved through the fog of men whose intentions she could only imagine and of women whose hard eyes suggested lives of desperation similar to what might await her. Carriages rattled past, their lamps creating momentary islands of light that exposed her vulnerability before plunging her back into concealing darkness.

Elizabeth walked until her legs ached and her lungs burned from the cold, damp air. When exhaustion finally forced her to stop, she found herself in a neighbourhood she didn't recognise with narrow buildings crowded together, washing strung between windows, and the smell of poverty hanging in the air as distinctly as the fog.

A church loomed ahead, its stone steps offering the only shelter visible in the gloom. Elizabeth sank down in the doorway, pulling her knees to her chest for warmth, her small bundle clutched protectively against her body.

Tomorrow, she would need to find food, seek safer shelter, perhaps look for work, though who would hire a girl with no references, no experience, and the shadow of her father's crimes potentially following her. But those were concerns for daylight. For now, survival meant simply enduring until morning.

As the church bell tolled midnight, Elizabeth huddled in her inadequate coat, one hand clutching her mother's locket, the other wrapped around the small knife she had taken from the kitchen, her only protection against the dangers that surrounded her.

She had escaped Veronica's immediate threat only to face the broader peril of London's uncaring streets. Whether she had improved her chances of survival or merely exchanged one form of danger for another remained to be seen.

The fog swirled around the church steps, obscuring her small figure from passersby. Elizabeth closed her eyes, not to sleep, she dared not lower her guard so completely, but to gather strength for whatever challenges tomorrow would bring. She was alone now, truly alone, with nothing but her wits and courage to sustain her.

The life she had known, however flawed, lay behind her. What awaited remained shrouded in uncertainty as impenetrable as the London fog.

CHAPTER 7

The cold stone of the church steps had leached all warmth from Elizabeth's body by dawn. She awoke with a jolt, neck stiff and limbs numb, momentarily disoriented until memory flooded back: Veronica's drunken rage, the pistol gleaming in lamplight, her own desperate flight into the London night.

Three men stood at the bottom of the steps, regarding her with predatory interest. Unshaven, clothes ragged but with the solid build of labourers rather than the gaunt look of the truly destitute, they spoke in low voices while eyeing her small bundle.

"Wot you got there, girl?" The largest of the three mounted the first step. "Looks like somethin' worth sharin'."

Elizabeth clutched her bundle tighter, heart hammering against her ribs. Her other hand slipped into her coat pocket, fingers closing around the kitchen knife she'd stolen during her escape.

"Nothing of value," she said, struggling to keep her voice steady. "Just some clothing."

The men exchanged glances, clearly disbelieving. The one on the steps advanced further.

"Posh voice for a girl sleepin' rough," he observed. "Runaway, are ya? From some fine house with plenty worth takin', I'd wager."

Elizabeth rose to her feet, back pressed against the heavy church door. Three against one—impossible odds even if she hadn't been weakened by cold and hunger.

"I have nothing worth stealing," she repeated, more firmly. "And the constable patrols this street regularly."

A lie, but delivered with enough conviction to make the men hesitate. The moment of uncertainty was all she needed. Elizabeth darted sideways, leaping down the steps and racing past the startled men before they could grab her.

"Get 'er!" one shouted, but Elizabeth had already rounded the corner, her bundle clutched to her chest, feet pounding against the cobblestones.

She ran blindly through streets still shrouded in early morning fog, turning randomly at corners until certain she'd lost her pursuers. Only then did she slow, lungs burning from the cold air and exertion.

The encounter had taught her the first harsh lesson of street life: sleeping in visible locations invited danger. Tonight, she would need to find somewhere more concealed, though where exactly remained a mystery in this unfamiliar part of London.

More immediate concerns pressed upon her as her stomach growled painfully. Elizabeth had last eaten yesterday morning, before Veronica's murderous outburst. The few coins in her pocket might buy bread, but she needed to conserve her meagre resources until she found some means of supporting herself.

Work. That was her most urgent need. With her education and refined manners, surely someone would hire her for respectable employment. A shop, perhaps, or as a nursery governess in a modest household.

As the city awakened around her, Elizabeth straightened her rumpled clothing, smoothed her hair, and prepared to present herself as a respectable girl seeking honest work rather than a desperate fugitive.

"References?" The milliner peered at Elizabeth over wire-rimmed spectacles, taking in her increasingly dishevelled appearance.

"I'm afraid my previous situation ended... abruptly," Elizabeth replied, trying to maintain her composure despite the woman's obvious suspicion. "But I'm well-educated and quick to learn. My needlework is excellent."

"No girl of quality finds herself without employment and references." The woman's tone hardened. "Unless there was some impropriety. Was there impropriety, miss?"

"No, madam. My father's circumstances changed, and I must now support myself."

"Your father's name?"

Elizabeth hesitated. The Flanders name, once respectable, now carried the taint of criminal notoriety. "I would prefer not to say."

The milliner's lips thinned. "As I suspected. Good day to you."

This marked her fourth rejection that morning. Each interview followed the same pattern: initial interest in her obvious education and refined speech, followed by suspicion when she could provide neither references nor a plausible explanation for her circumstances.

By afternoon, hunger had become a constant companion, a gnawing emptiness unlike anything Elizabeth had experienced in her previously comfortable life. She had ventured into progressively less respectable neighbourhoods, approaching shops and businesses that might have lower standards for employment, but her accent and manner worked against her. She was neither fish nor fowl; too refined for manual labour, too suspicious for respectable positions.

A bakery's aroma nearly overwhelmed her as she passed. Elizabeth paused, calculating whether she could spare a few precious pennies for a small loaf. The mental arithmetic was interrupted by a passing woman who bumped her roughly.

"Move along," the woman hissed. "Your sort ain't welcome here."

Elizabeth stumbled away, confused by the hostility until she caught sight of her reflection in a shop window. Three days without proper washing facilities had left her face smudged and her hair tangled. Her once-neat clothing now hung crumpled and stained. She looked not like a genteel girl seeking employment but a vagrant, or worse, the sort of woman who sold herself on street corners.

No wonder doors closed at her approach. Her appearance contradicted her speech, creating an inconsistency that aroused suspicion rather than sympathy.

Night was falling, her second on the streets, and Elizabeth had accomplished nothing beyond exhausting herself with fruitless inquiries. She had no food, no shelter, and no prospect of either. The few coins in her pocket seemed increasingly precious as her options dwindled.

She found temporary refuge in an alley behind a public house, huddled between barrels that offered some protection from the wind. Sleep came in fitful bursts, interrupted by the cold, by drunken patrons stumbling into the alley to relieve themselves, and by her own growling stomach.

By dawn of her third day as a fugitive, Elizabeth faced the reality that conventional employment remained closed to her without references or a plausible story. Her hunger had progressed beyond discomfort to a constant, painful emptiness that made thinking difficult.

She would need to spend some of her dwindling

coins on food or risk collapse. But as she approached a market stall selling day-old bread at reduced prices, Elizabeth's gaze fell upon a momentarily unattended tray of fresh rolls. The vendor was turned away, arguing with another customer over proper change.

The thought formed before she could suppress it: she could simply take one. Just one small roll to quiet the worst pangs of hunger.

Her hand moved almost of its own accord, reaching out as she passed the stall, fingers closing around a warm roll and slipping it into her coat pocket in one smooth motion.

Three steps past the stall, a meaty hand clamped onto her arm.

"Thief!" the vendor bellowed, his face reddening with anger as he spun her around. "Thought I didn't see you, did you? Filthy little pickpocket!"

Elizabeth froze, the stolen roll burning like a coal in her pocket. Around her, the market crowd turned to stare, their faces a blur of curiosity and condemnation.

"I'm sorry," she stammered. "I was hungry—I'll pay—"

"Pay with what?" The man yanked her closer, his breath hot against her face. "Empty pockets, I'd wager. Jenkins! Call the constable!"

"Please," Elizabeth begged, true panic rising in her throat. If arrested, she might be recognised as William Flanders' daughter. Worse, Veronica might learn of her capture and find a way to finish what she'd started. "I've never stolen before, I was desperate—"

"Save your tales for the magistrate." The vendor's grip tightened painfully. "They'll have you in the workhouse or transported, and good riddance."

With strength born of terror, Elizabeth wrenched her arm free and bolted through the crowded market. Behind her, shouts rose as the vendor gave chase, joined by others responding to cries of "Stop, thief!"

Elizabeth darted between stalls, knocked aside a basket of apples, and sprinted toward the maze of side streets beyond the market. Her lungs burned, her legs wobbled from weakness, but fear drove her forward.

Rounding a corner at full speed, she collided hard with someone coming the opposite direction. The impact knocked her backwards onto the cobble-stones, her small bundle flying from her grasp.

Rough hands seized her shoulders before she could scramble away.

"Wotcher think you're doing?" a young man's

voice demanded, his grip firm but not brutal. "Trying to pick my pocket, was you?"

Elizabeth looked up into a lean face with sharp, assessing eyes. The young man appeared to be perhaps eighteen, dressed in patched but clean clothing, his sandy hair cut short in a practical style. His expression showed suspicion rather than malice.

"No! I'm running from—" Elizabeth broke off as shouts from the market grew closer. "Please, they'll arrest me—"

Understanding flickered in the young man's eyes. He glanced toward the approaching voices, then made a swift decision.

"This way," he said, releasing her shoulders to grab her bundle with one hand and her arm with the other. "Quick, if you don't want to be caught."

He pulled her into a narrow passage between buildings, barely wide enough for them to move single file. They emerged into a warren of back alleys that twisted away from the market district, the young man leading with the confidence of one who knew every shortcut and hiding place.

Only when the sounds of pursuit had faded completely did he slow, guiding Elizabeth into the shelter of a recessed doorway.

"What did you nick?" he asked without preamble.

Elizabeth hesitated, then withdrew the now-squashed roll from her pocket.

The young man stared at it, then at her face, something shifting in his expression. "All this chase for a penny roll?"

"I was hungry," Elizabeth said simply.

He studied her more carefully, taking in details his initial suspicion had overlooked: her speech, the quality of her coat despite its rumpled state, and the incongruity of her obvious refinement and her current desperation.

"You're no street girl," he said. "What's your story, then?"

Before Elizabeth could answer, a wave of dizziness swept over her. Three days of minimal food and water, sleepless nights in the cold, and the exertion of her flight combined to overwhelm her weakened body. She swayed on her feet, darkness crowding the edges of her vision.

The young man caught her as her knees buckled, his expression changing from suspicion to concern.

"Blimey, you're half-starved," he muttered. "When did you last eat proper?"

"Day before yesterday," Elizabeth whispered, struggling to remain conscious. "Morning."

He swore under his breath, then made another

swift decision. "Can you walk if I help you? Got a place not far. Safer than here."

Elizabeth nodded weakly, allowing him to support her weight as they moved through increasingly dilapidated streets. She should have been frightened, placing herself at the mercy of an unknown man in this dangerous part of London, but hunger and exhaustion had overwhelmed caution. Besides, some instinct told her this rough-spoken young man meant her no harm.

They reached an abandoned warehouse, its windows boarded, its brick facade crumbling in places. The young man led her to a side entrance concealed behind piled crates, producing a key to unlock a heavy padlock.

"Mind your step," he warned as they entered a cavernous space filled with shadows. "Follow me exact."

Elizabeth stumbled after him, noting how he navigated the debris-strewn floor with practised ease, avoiding weak spots and obstacles without needing to look. They climbed a set of rickety stairs to a small room that had once been an office or storeroom.

Here, the young man had created a surprisingly

orderly living space. A pallet lay in one corner with neatly folded blankets. Crates served as furniture. A small brazier held carefully banked coals. Shelves fashioned from scavenged wood contained tins, jars, and other supplies arranged with military precision.

"Sit," he directed, pointing to a crate covered with a relatively clean cloth. "Before you fall."

Elizabeth sank down gratefully, watching as he rekindled the brazier's coals and set a small pot of water to heat. From a tin, he extracted hard biscuits, breaking one in half and offering her the larger portion.

"Eat slow," he advised as she reached for it with trembling hands. "Too fast when you're empty and you'll sick it back up."

The biscuit was dry and tasteless, but Elizabeth had never appreciated food more. She forced herself to take small bites, chewing thoroughly before swallowing, while the young man prepared tea in a dented pot.

"Thank you," she said when she'd finished her portion. "I don't know your name."

"Bob," he replied, pouring the tea into two chipped cups. "Bob Miller."

"I'm Elizabeth Flanders."

His hand froze in the act of passing her the tea. "Flanders? William Flanders' daughter?"

Elizabeth tensed, suddenly alert despite her exhaustion. "You know my father?"

Bob's expression hardened. "Know of him. Everyone in certain circles does." He set the tea down with deliberate care. "The respectable merchant with his grave-robbing business. The man whose carelessness killed my father three years back."

The revelation struck Elizabeth like a physical blow. This wasn't random chance; the young man who'd helped her had a connection to her family, and not a positive one.

"Your father worked for mine?" she asked, trying to make sense of this new information.

"John Miller. One of William Flanders' diggers." Bob's voice remained controlled, but tension radiated from his rigid posture. "Crushed when a grave collapsed during excavation. Your father paid my mother some coins, less than he made selling my father's last 'specimens', then forgot us."

Elizabeth's mind raced despite her fatigue. Had Bob recognised her somehow? Was his assistance a prelude to revenge?

"Is that why you helped me? Because you knew who I was?"

Bob laughed without humour. "I had no idea who you were until you gave your name. Been tracking your family, true enough. Learning your father's methods, his contacts. Planning... something. Revenge, maybe. Or justice." He shrugged. "But finding you half-starved in the street wasn't part of any plan."

Elizabeth believed him. The surprise in his face when she'd revealed her identity had been genuine. Still, the coincidence seemed extraordinary.

"Why were you in that particular market today?" she asked.

"I work odd jobs there sometimes. Unloading crates, minding stalls." He studied her over the rim of his teacup. "The better question is why William Flanders' daughter is stealing bread and sleeping rough. Last I heard, your father was transported, but the family business continued."

The simple inquiry opened floodgates Elizabeth had been struggling to keep closed. Exhaustion, hunger, and the sheer relief of speaking to someone who already knew the worst about her family broke her careful composure.

"My father's new wife murdered my mother," she said bluntly. "Poisoned her over weeks while pretending to care for her illness. Then she betrayed my father to the authorities, arranged his transportation, and took control of everything. Three nights ago, she tried to murder me too, with my father's pistol, drunk and boasting about all her victims."

Bob's expression shifted from suspicion to something more complex; not quite sympathy, but a recognition of shared injury.

"So you ran," he said. It wasn't a question.

"With nothing but what I could carry." Elizabeth gestured to her small bundle. "I've been trying to find work, but no one will hire a girl without references who can't explain her circumstances."

"And you can hardly tell them the truth," Bob observed. "That your family makes its living from the dead."

The blunt assessment should have offended her, but Elizabeth was beyond such niceties. "Yes."

They sat in silence for several minutes, each absorbing the strange convergence of their circumstances. Outside, rain began to fall, drumming against the warehouse roof and trickling through cracks to form puddles on the floor below.

"You can stay tonight," Bob said finally. "Too wet to be outside, and you're in no state to travel far. Tomorrow, we'll see."

"Why help me?" Elizabeth asked. "If my father wronged your family—"

"Your father wronged my family," Bob interrupted. "Not you. And I'm not him, taking payment from the dead and leaving the living to suffer." He stood abruptly, moving to rearrange the blankets on his pallet. "You take the bed. I'll manage with these crates."

Elizabeth wanted to protest, but lacked the strength. The prospect of sleeping on something other than cold stone or hard ground overwhelmed her pride.

"Thank you," she said simply.

Bob nodded, then busied himself with practical matters such as securing the door, banking the brazier's coals, and arranging his makeshift bedding. Elizabeth removed her shoes but otherwise remained fully clothed as she lay down on the pallet, pulling the thin blankets around her.

The relative warmth and safety, combined with her extreme exhaustion, should have brought immediate sleep. Instead, her mind raced with the day's revelations. Bob Miller, son of a man who died in her father's employ, who had been tracking her family for reasons not fully explained, who had helped her despite every reason not to.

"Bob?" she asked softly, uncertain if he was still awake.

"Mm?" His voice came from the darkness where he lay on his improvised bed.

"How do you survive? I mean, what do you do for money?"

A pause. "Whatever's needed. Odd jobs mostly. Loading, unloading. Running messages. Some things best not discussed."

Elizabeth understood the implication. Legal employment sustained him partially, but other activities, perhaps pickpocketing or similar crimes, filled the gaps.

"I need to learn," she said. "How to survive out here. I can't go back, and no respectable household will hire me."

"Sleep," Bob replied. "We'll talk tomorrow."

But Elizabeth's mind continued working despite her body's desperate need for rest. Bob knew the street world she must now navigate. More importantly, he knew about her father's business and had been studying it, by his own admission.

Her father had taught her the organisation of the

resurrection trade, such as which medical schools paid best, how to identify valuable specimens, and the network of informants and grave diggers that kept the business functioning. Bob, through his father and his own investigations, knew the practical side, the actual exhumation, the physical skills needed, and the dangers to avoid.

Together, they possessed the complete knowledge needed to rebuild such an operation. The thought should have horrified her, given her previous reluctance to participate in her father's criminal activities. But three days of hunger and rejection had shifted Elizabeth's moral calculations. Survival now outweighed principle.

"We could work together," she said into the darkness, the idea taking shape as she spoke. "I know the business connections, which doctors pay, what they look for, and how to approach them. You know the practical side, the streets, how to avoid detection."

Silence greeted her suggestion. For a moment, Elizabeth thought Bob had fallen asleep or was ignoring her. Then his voice came, cautious but not dismissive.

"That's grave talk for a girl raised in comfort. You suggesting we become resurrection men?"

"I'm suggesting we use what we know to survive,"

Elizabeth replied. "Unless you have a better proposal for two people with no respectable options. Resurrectionists," she corrected.

Another long pause. "Sleep," Bob said finally. "Your mind's not right from hunger. We'll speak of this when you're stronger."

Elizabeth wanted to press the point but recognised the wisdom in his words. Her body demanded rest, her mind clarity that only food and sleep could restore. The ethical implications of her proposal could wait until basic needs were met.

She closed her eyes, listening to the rain drumming on the roof and Bob's steady breathing across the room. For the first time since fleeing Veronica's murderous rage, Elizabeth felt something beyond terror and desperation: a fragile hope that survival might be possible after all.

Not through the respectable channels she had fruitlessly pursued, but through an alliance with this unexpected companion who shared her knowledge of death's profitable secrets. The irony didn't escape her that her father's criminal legacy might now provide her only path forward, and that the son of a man William Flanders had carelessly sacrificed might become her partner in this grim enterprise.

As sleep finally claimed her, Elizabeth's last

coherent thought was that her father would appreciate the symmetry of it all: his daughter and his victim's son, united by the business of the dead that had destroyed both their families.

Elizabeth woke to grey morning light filtering through cracks in the boarded windows. For a moment, disorientation gripped her, the unfamiliar surroundings, the hard pallet beneath her, and the smell of damp stone and coal smoke. Then memory returned: fleeing from Veronica, days of hunger and rejection, her collision with Bob Miller, and their strange conversation about shared knowledge and possible partnership.

She sat up, wincing as stiff muscles protested the movement. The warehouse room was empty, Bob's makeshift bedding neatly folded on a crate. Had he abandoned her? The thought sent a spike of panic through Elizabeth until she noticed the small fire in the brazier and a cup of water placed within easy reach.

As she sipped the water gratefully, the door creaked open. Bob entered carrying a small bundle wrapped in newspaper.

"You're awake," he observed unnecessarily. "Brought breakfast."

He unwrapped the package to reveal a half loaf of

bread, a small piece of cheese, and an apple. By the standards of Elizabeth's former life, it was a pauper's meal. In her current circumstances, it seemed a feast.

"Where did you get this?" she asked as he divided the food, giving her the larger portions.

"Market. Day-old bread's cheap first thing." He didn't elaborate on whether the food had been purchased or acquired through other means. "Eat slow, remember."

They shared the simple meal in silence. Elizabeth found the bread easier to digest than yesterday's hard biscuit, although she still had to force herself not to bolt it down like a starving animal. With food in her stomach and a night's sleep behind her, her mind worked more clearly.

"About what I said last night," she began.

"About becoming resurrection men... resurrectionists?" Bob corrected himself, his direct approach startling her. "Thought you might regret that in the morning light."

"I don't," Elizabeth said, surprising herself with her certainty. "It wasn't just hunger talking. We both know the business from different angles. Together, we have the complete knowledge needed to make it work."

Bob studied her with those sharp, assessing eyes

that seemed to see beyond surface appearances. "It's dangerous work. Illegal. If caught, you'd face transportation like your father, or worse, being a woman in such a trade."

"I'm already living illegally," Elizabeth pointed out. "No fixed address, no legitimate employment, stealing food to survive. At least this would be something I understand."

"You understand the theory," Bob corrected. "The business side your father handled from his comfortable office. The actual work, digging in all weather, handling the dead, carrying bodies through the night, that's different."

"I can learn," Elizabeth insisted. "I'm stronger than I look."

Bob's expression remained sceptical. "Why this? Why not something less... grim?"

Elizabeth considered the question seriously. "Because it's the only valuable skill I possess. My education, my manners, my background, none of that helps me now. But I know which medical schools pay best for which specimens. I know how to approach doctors without arousing suspicion. I understand the business in ways most resurrection men don't."

She leaned forward, intensity overcoming her

usual reserve. "And you know the practical side: how to identify which graves are worth opening, how to work quietly, how to transport specimens without detection. Your father taught you, didn't he? Before he died."

Bob's jaw tightened at the mention of his father, but he nodded slowly. "Some. And I've learned more since, watching other gangs work."

"Then we have everything we need except tools and capital," Elizabeth said. "And those can be acquired."

"It's not that simple," Bob argued, though with less conviction than before. "We'd need connections, informants at the cemeteries, proper equipment."

"I know which connections matter. As for informants and equipment, we start small and build." Elizabeth could see that her logic was affecting him. "One successful delivery to the right doctor would fund the next operation. That's how all such businesses grow."

Bob fell silent, turning the proposal over in his mind. Elizabeth waited, recognising this moment as pivotal. If he refused, she would be alone again, facing London's streets with no skills, no shelter, and dwindling options.

"A week," he said finally. "Stay here, regain your

strength. Learn some basic street survival. If you still want this path after seeing what life out here is truly like, then maybe."

It wasn't agreement, but it wasn't rejection either. Elizabeth nodded, accepting the compromise. "A week."

"First lesson," Bob said, rising to his feet. "We need water. There's a pump three streets over. You'll carry one bucket, I'll manage two."

Such a mundane task, fetching water, yet Elizabeth recognised it as the beginning of her education in this new world. No servants, no conveniences, just the daily labour required to sustain life at its most basic level.

As they descended the warehouse stairs, buckets in hand, Elizabeth glanced at her unlikely companion. The son of a man her father had treated as expendable, now her only ally in a hostile world. The irony wasn't lost on her, nor was the precariousness of their arrangement.

But for the first time since fleeing into the London night, Elizabeth felt something beyond fear and desperation. This strange partnership, born of shared knowledge of death's profitable secrets, offered a path forward; morally compromised, dangerous, uncertain, but a path nonetheless.

Whether it led to survival or destruction remained to be seen. For now, she would focus on the immediate task: learning to carry water without spilling it, the first of many lessons in her new life as a girl of the streets.

CHAPTER 8

"Your father didn't just employ mine," Bob said, breaking the week's unspoken agreement to avoid discussing William Flanders. "He was training him as his lieutenant."

Elizabeth looked up from the torn shirt she was mending. A week of regular meals and shelter had restored some colour to her cheeks, though she remained thinner than she'd been in the Flanders household. The warehouse room had become familiar, almost comfortable, as she learned the rhythms of Bob's spartan existence.

"What do you mean?" she asked, setting aside her sewing.

Bob leaned against the wall, arms crossed. "My

father wasn't just a digger. He knew which cemeteries had the weakest security, which medical schools paid the best prices, and how to identify fresh graves worth robbing." His voice remained neutral, but Elizabeth detected an undercurrent of pride. "Your father was teaching him everything: the entire network of fences, informants, and corrupt officials that make the trade possible."

"I didn't know," Elizabeth said truthfully. Her father had rarely discussed individual members of his resurrection gang.

"When my father died, I lost more than family. I lost my future." Bob's expression hardened. "Your father had been preparing him, and by extension, me, to eventually take over portions of the operation."

Understanding dawned. "That's why you've been tracking my family. Not just for revenge—"

"For knowledge," Bob finished. "I possessed half of what's needed to rebuild the operation. Your father had the other half: his contacts and methods."

"And now I have that half," Elizabeth said slowly, the pieces falling into place. Their meeting hadn't been mere chance. Bob had been gathering intelligence about the Flanders business for years, positioning himself to eventually claim what he saw as his inheritance. "Is that why you helped me? Because you realised who I was?"

Bob shook his head. "I told you true. I had no idea who you were when we collided. But once I knew..." He shrugged. "It seemed like fate, perhaps. Or just London's peculiar way of bringing the right people together at the right time."

Elizabeth studied him, reassessing their relationship in light of this revelation. "So you'll do it? Partner with me in rebuilding the business?"

"One operation," Bob said, caution evident in his tone. "We try once, see if you can stomach the actual work. It's one thing to talk about resurrection men from the safety of a respectable home. It's another to dig up the dead with your own hands."

Elizabeth nodded, accepting the challenge. "When?"

"Tomorrow night. I've been watching a small cemetery in Southwark. Poor security, recent burial that won't have started significant decomposition." Bob's practical assessment made Elizabeth's stomach tighten, but she kept her expression neutral. "We'll need tools."

"What sort?"

"Shovels, obviously. A crowbar for the coffin. Sacks for transport." He assessed her thoughtfully.

"And dark clothing. That coat's too noticeable, even at night."

Elizabeth glanced at her once-fine coat, now shabby from sleeping rough but still clearly of better quality than most in this neighbourhood. "I can trade it, perhaps."

"We'll find something suitable," Bob agreed. "For now, let's discuss the cemetery layout."

He produced a crude map drawn on scavenged paper, spreading it across a crate. Elizabeth moved closer, noting the methodical detail of walls, gates, the watchman's route, and recent burial locations.

"You've been planning this for some time," she observed.

"Considering it," Bob corrected. "Never had the right connections to make it worthwhile. Medical schools don't buy from just anyone off the street. They prefer established suppliers."

"That's where I help," Elizabeth said. "St. Bartholomew's Hospital. My father mentioned a Dr. Pemberton who handles acquisitions. He prefers to deal with intermediaries who present themselves properly."

Bob nodded appreciatively. "Your father's connections with proper credentials. My knowledge of the practical work. Together, we might actually succeed."

As they bent over the map, planning their macabre expedition, Elizabeth felt a strange mixture of emotions: apprehension at the grim task ahead, determination to prove herself capable, and an unexpected sense of purpose after days of aimless survival. This partnership, however unconventional, gave her a path forward when all others had closed.

Whether she could actually dig up a grave and handle a corpse remained to be seen. But the alternative of returning to the streets alone was unthinkable.

* * *

THE CEMETERY LOOMED BEFORE THEM, its iron gates locked for the night, its stone walls silhouetted against the cloudy sky. Elizabeth's borrowed clothes, a boy's shirt, trousers, and cap that concealed her hair, felt strange against her skin, but provided better mobility than her dress would have allowed. The rough wool jacket Bob had procured from somewhere smelled of previous owners but offered protection against the November chill.

"This way," Bob whispered, leading her toward a section of wall partially hidden by overgrown yew trees. "The stones are loose here. I checked yesterday."

Elizabeth followed, carrying a canvas sack while Bob managed the shovels, makeshift tools he'd acquired through means she hadn't questioned. The wall proved easier to climb than she'd expected, with convenient footholds where mortar had crumbled away. They dropped down inside the cemetery, landing softly on damp grass.

The silence pressed against Elizabeth's ears, broken only by the distant sounds of London's night traffic and the occasional rustle of leaves. Gravestones stretched in uneven rows, some grand and ornate, others simple markers. The moon emerged briefly from behind clouds, casting everything in silvery light that made the scene both beautiful and eerie.

"Stay close," Bob murmured. "Watchman makes rounds every hour but keeps to the main paths. Our target's this way."

He moved with surprising confidence through the maze of graves, avoiding the gravel paths in favour of the silent grass between plots. Elizabeth followed, her heart pounding so loudly she feared it might alert the watchman despite his distance.

They reached a fresh grave marked with a simple wooden cross. "James Wilson, 1820-1852, Rest in Peace" read the temporary marker. A proper headstone would come later, after the ground had settled, if the occupant remained undisturbed that long.

"Recent burial," Bob whispered, kneeling to assess the turned earth. "Three days ago. Ground's still loose, which makes our work easier."

He handed Elizabeth a shovel, and reality crashed upon her. Until this moment, their plan had existed in the abstract as discussions of logistics, security, and potential profits. Now, faced with an actual grave and the prospect of disturbing someone's final rest, the moral weight of their intended action struck her fully.

"I..." she hesitated, the shovel heavy in her hands.

"Having second thoughts?" Bob asked, not unkindly. "No shame in it. We can leave now, try to find another way."

Elizabeth stared at the grave, considering their options. Legitimate employment remained closed to her without references. Begging or prostitution, the common fates of desperate women, offered nothing but degradation and eventual destruction. Theft might sustain them temporarily, but it carried risks as great as their current enterprise with fewer rewards.

"No," she said finally, gripping the shovel more firmly. "Let's proceed."

Bob nodded, respecting her decision without comment. "I'll start. Watch how I do it; quiet and methodical. No wasted motion."

He began removing earth from the grave, his movements indeed economical and practised. Elizabeth joined him after observing his technique, finding the physical labour more demanding than she'd anticipated. Blisters formed on her palms despite the cloth wrappings Bob had provided for her hands. Her back protested the unaccustomed strain. But she continued, matching her rhythm to Bob's, determined to prove herself capable.

They worked in silence, broken only by their controlled breathing and the soft sound of shovels cutting through soil. The grave was thankfully shallow, being a pauper's burial rather than the deeper excavation a wealthier family would have commissioned. Within an hour, they had removed enough earth to expose the rough pine coffin beneath.

"Now comes the difficult part," Bob whispered, producing a crowbar from his jacket. "The lid needs to be pried open. Sometimes they splinter or make noise. Be ready to run if necessary."

Elizabeth nodded, wiping sweat from her forehead despite the cold night air. Bob worked the crowbar under the coffin lid, applying steady pressure until the nails began to give way with low creaks that seemed thunderous in the cemetery silence. A final push, and the lid lifted enough to reveal what lay within.

The smell hit Elizabeth first, not the overwhelming stench of advanced decay, but something subtler and somehow worse: the sweet-sour odour of a body beginning its transition to dust. She turned her head away, fighting the urge to vomit.

"Breathe through your mouth," Bob advised quietly. "It helps."

He lifted the lid further, exposing the corpse fully to the moonlight. James Wilson had been a man of perhaps thirty, his features still recognisable in death, though his skin had taken on the waxy pallor characteristic of the recently deceased. He wore simple burial clothes: a clean shirt and trousers that represented his family's best effort at dignity in death.

"Good condition," Bob assessed clinically. "No

visible disease. Medical schools prefer specimens without advanced decay or disfigurement."

Elizabeth forced herself to look, to see the "specimen" as Bob did and as her father had, as merchandise rather than a person. It was the only way she could continue.

"How do we... remove him?" she asked, her voice steadier than she felt.

"I'll lift from the shoulders. You take the feet," Bob instructed. "We transfer him to the sack, then refill the grave enough to hide our work. The groundskeeper will attribute any sunken earth to natural settling."

Elizabeth positioned herself at the foot of the coffin, steeling herself for the moment of contact. When Bob nodded, she reached in and grasped the corpse's ankles through the thin fabric of his burial clothes. The chill of the flesh penetrated her cloth-wrapped hands, sending a shudder through her body.

Together, they lifted James Wilson from his coffin, the dead weight more substantial than Elizabeth had expected. As they manoeuvred him into the waiting sack, his arm swung limply, brushing against Elizabeth's wrist. The contact, though brief, sent another wave of revulsion through her, but she maintained her grip, focusing on the task rather than its moral implications.

Once the body was secured in the sack, they began refilling the grave, working as quickly as prudence allowed. Elizabeth's muscles screamed in protest, but fear and determination drove her forward. The empty coffin disappeared beneath the soil, the grave gradually resuming its original appearance, although with slightly sunken earth that might indeed be attributed to natural settling.

"We need to smooth the surface," Bob whispered, using the flat of his shovel to erase obvious signs of disturbance. "Make it look undisturbed to casual inspection."

Elizabeth followed his example, patting down the soil and arranging it to match the surrounding graves. They had nearly finished when a lantern light appeared on the main path, swinging gently as the night watchman made his rounds.

"Don't move," Bob hissed, dropping flat behind a neighbouring headstone.

Elizabeth froze, then slowly sank to the ground, pressing herself against the damp earth beside their macabre package. Her heart pounded so violently she feared the watchman might hear it from thirty yards away.

The lantern paused at the cemetery crossroads. The watchman appeared to be consulting a pocket watch, his silhouette visible against the yellow light. For a terrible moment, Elizabeth thought he might leave the path to check this section more thoroughly. Instead, after a brief hesitation, he continued his circuit, the light gradually receding toward the opposite end of the cemetery.

"That was too close," Bob breathed when the watchman had disappeared from view. "We need to move now, before he circles back."

They gathered their tools and the sack containing James Wilson's mortal remains, making their way back to the cemetery wall with greater urgency than caution. Getting the body over the wall proved challenging with the dead weight requiring both of them to lift and manoeuvre, but they managed without dropping their grim cargo or making enough noise to alert the watchman.

Once outside the cemetery, they faced the next challenge: transporting the body through London's streets without arousing suspicion. Bob had prepared for this, leading Elizabeth through a series of back alleys and service passages where late-night pedestrians were rare and those they did encounter were unlikely to question two figures carrying a heavy sack.

"We can't take him to the hospital tonight," Bob explained as they stashed their burden in a secure corner of the warehouse. "Medical schools don't accept specimens at this hour. It would draw attention."

"What about..." Elizabeth gestured toward the sack, unable to complete the question.

"The cold will preserve him well enough until morning," Bob replied, understanding her concern. "We'll approach St. Bartholomew's at first light, when deliveries of all sorts arrive and one more package won't attract notice."

Elizabeth nodded, grateful for the delay that would allow her to compose herself before the next phase of their operation. Her hands still felt contaminated from touching the corpse, and she scrubbed them repeatedly in the bucket of water Bob provided, though the sensation of death lingered on her skin.

They slept little that night, both too alert with the nervous energy that follows a dangerous endeavour and too aware of their silent companion in the corner. Elizabeth dozed fitfully, waking from dreams in which James Wilson sat up in his sack and asked why she had disturbed his rest.

Dawn found them approaching the rear entrance of St. Bartholomew's Hospital, their burden now concealed in a crate borrowed from the warehouse and loaded onto a handcart. Elizabeth had changed back into her dress, though she kept the borrowed jacket for warmth. Her appearance, while still far from her former neatness, had been improved with Bob's help, her hair combed and pinned, face washed, and mud cleaned from her shoes.

"Remember," Bob murmured as they neared the delivery entrance, "you do the talking. Your accent and manner will open doors, my appearance would leave closed."

Elizabeth nodded, trying to project a confidence she didn't feel. She had observed her father's business interactions for years but had never conducted such negotiations herself. The stakes were enormous; if rejected by the hospital, they would have risked grave robbery for nothing and would still have a corpse to dispose of somehow.

The delivery area bustled with morning activity, with carts bringing food, linens, medical supplies, and other necessities for the hospital's daily operation. Bob positioned their handcart among the others, looking like any delivery boy waiting his turn. Elizabeth approached a harried-looking porter who appeared to be directing the flow of goods.

"Excuse me," she said, her refined accent immediately drawing his attention. "I have a delivery for Dr. Pemberton. A private matter."

The porter assessed her with the quick judgment of one accustomed to determining who deserved immediate attention. Elizabeth's speech and bearing, despite her modest clothing, apparently passed his test.

"Dr. Pemberton doesn't usually receive deliveries here," he said, lowering his voice. "Unless it's... special materials?"

"Precisely," Elizabeth confirmed, matching his discreet tone. "My associate and I have brought what he requested. For anatomical study."

Understanding dawned in the porter's eyes. He was clearly familiar with the hospital's less public acquisitions. "Wait here," he instructed, disappearing through a side door.

Minutes later, a tall, distinguished man with silver hair and spectacles emerged. His surgical apron bore stains that Elizabeth preferred not to identify.

"I am Dr. Pemberton," he said, studying Elizabeth

with professional detachment. "Porter says you have materials for me?"

"Yes, Doctor." Elizabeth maintained the calm demeanour she'd observed in her father's business dealings. "A male specimen, approximately thirty years of age, excellent condition. Obtained last night."

The doctor's eyebrows rose slightly at her clinical description. Few women involved in the resurrection trade spoke so directly or knowledgeably.

"Let me see," he said, moving toward the handcart where Bob waited impassively.

Dr. Pemberton examined their offering with the critical eye of a butcher assessing meat. He checked the body's condition, flexibility of limbs, and absence of visible disease. Elizabeth watched, forcing herself to view the transaction as purely commercial despite the moral implications that threatened to overwhelm her.

"Acceptable," he pronounced finally. "Though not exceptional. Four pounds."

Elizabeth had anticipated this negotiation. "The freshness and condition warrant at least six," she countered. "The subject has been deceased less than four days."

"Five pounds," Dr. Pemberton offered. "And

potential for regular business if your... acquisitions maintain this quality."

Elizabeth glanced at Bob, who gave an almost imperceptible nod. "Agreed," she said. "Five pounds."

The transaction concluded quickly after that. Money changed hands, the crate was transferred to hospital porters who knew better than to ask questions, and Elizabeth and Bob found themselves walking away from St. Bartholomew's five pounds richer. It was more money than either had seen in months.

They maintained professional composure until they reached a small, deserted square several streets from the hospital. Only then did Elizabeth allow her carefully constructed facade to crumble. She sank onto a bench, her entire body trembling with delayed reaction to what they had done.

"We sold a man," she whispered, the full weight of their actions finally breaking through her pragmatic detachment. "We dug up James Wilson and sold him like... like merchandise."

Bob sat beside her, close but not touching, respecting the privacy of her moral crisis. "We did," he agreed simply. "No point pretending otherwise."

"I saw my mother's face," Elizabeth admitted, the confession tearing from her throat. "When we lifted him from the coffin. For a moment, he was my mother, and we were violating someone's rest just as someone might have violated hers."

Bob remained silent, allowing her to process the horror and guilt that had been building since they first opened the coffin.

"Does it get easier?" she asked finally, looking up at him with eyes that had seen too much for her fifteen years.

"Yes," Bob said. Then, with brutal honesty, "That's perhaps the worst part. It does get easier, and that change in yourself is another kind of horror."

Elizabeth nodded, understanding exactly what he meant. The ability to distance oneself from the moral implications of such work required a hardening of the soul that represented its own kind of death.

"My father justified it as serving medical science," she said quietly. "Helping doctors learn to save the living by studying the dead."

"There's truth in that," Bob acknowledged. "These specimens do teach doctors their craft. My father believed that, even as he acknowledged the wrongness of disturbing graves." He gestured toward the hospital behind them. "Without bodies to study, how many more patients would die under unskilled hands?"

The rationalisation offered small comfort, but Elizabeth clung to it nonetheless. "We needed to eat," she added. "To survive."

"Yes." Bob's simple agreement carried neither judgment nor absolution. "That's the choice we made."

They sat in silence for several minutes, the weight of their new partnership now sealed with a successful operation, settling between them. Finally, Elizabeth straightened her shoulders, wiping away tears she hadn't realised she'd shed.

"What now?" she asked.

"Now we find safer lodgings," Bob replied practically. "The warehouse serves as a temporary shelter, but we need somewhere more secure to store equipment and plan operations. Somewhere with a proper lock and perhaps a landlord who doesn't ask too many questions."

Elizabeth nodded, grateful for his focus on immediate practicalities rather than the larger moral questions they both needed time to process. "And we'll need better tools. The makeshift shovels were barely adequate."

"Proper grave robbing tools," Bob agreed. "Designed for quiet, efficient work."

"I know which cemeteries have the weakest security," Elizabeth offered, drawing on her father's knowledge. "And which medical schools pay best for specific types of specimens."

They were discussing business now, their brief moment of moral reflection set aside in favour of survival planning. Elizabeth recognised this as another form of coping, focusing on the practical aspects of their work rather than its ethical implications.

As they walked away from the square, five pounds secure in Bob's inner pocket, Elizabeth acknowledged the transformation that had begun. She had crossed a line, becoming something her former self would have viewed with horror: a resurrection woman, trafficking in the dead for profit. A resurrectionist in every way.

Yet she had also survived when all other paths closed to her. The money they'd earned would provide food, shelter, and the means to continue this grim enterprise with greater safety and efficiency. The resurrection trade had claimed her, just as it had claimed her father before her, though through different circumstances and choices.

"We'll need to establish a reputation for reliability," she said as they navigated the morning crowds. "Quality specimens, discreet delivery, reasonable prices. That's how my father built his business."

"And we'll need to avoid Crowe's territory," Bob added. "His gang controls the major cemeteries in the eastern districts. Trespassers face consequences worse than legal prosecution."

Elizabeth absorbed this information, adding it to her growing understanding of London's resurrection underworld. They were the smallest of operators now, but with her business knowledge and Bob's practical skills, they might eventually build something substantial. A partnership born of desperation but sustained by complementary abilities.

When they turned toward a neighbourhood of modest lodging houses where they might find suitable accommodations, Elizabeth caught her reflection in a shop window. The face that looked back seemed older, harder than it had been just days ago, the face of someone who had made difficult choices and would make more in the days to come.

She was no longer merely William Flanders' daughter, but something new and undefined: a young woman carving her own path through

London's darkest trade, with only her wits and her unlikely partnership with Bob Miller to sustain her.

The irony wasn't lost on her. Her father's criminal legacy, which she had once viewed with horror and reluctance, had become her salvation in ways she could never have anticipated. Whether that salvation would ultimately prove a curse remained to be seen.

For now, she had survived her first resurrection operation. Tomorrow would bring new challenges, new moral compromises, and perhaps a growing hardness that both protected and diminished her. But it would also bring another day of life when death, either at Veronica's hands or through starvation on London's streets, had seemed her only future.

Elizabeth squared her shoulders and followed Bob toward their next destination, leaving behind the girl she had been and embracing, however reluctantly, the resurrection woman she was becoming.

CHAPTER 9

Elizabeth smoothed her skirts as she entered the churchyard, her posture deliberately refined despite the modest quality of her clothes. The groundskeeper, a weathered man with dirt permanently embedded in the creases of his hands, touched his cap in reflexive deference to her apparent social standing.

"Good afternoon," she greeted him, her accent carrying the unmistakable polish of proper education. "I'm inquiring about arrangements for my late uncle. The family wishes to ensure appropriate placement."

The groundskeeper, Murphy, according to Bob's information, straightened slightly. "South section's where the better plots are, miss. Though they come at a premium."

"Money is no object for a proper Christian burial," Elizabeth replied, opening her reticule to extract a half crown that represented far more than information was typically worth. "I understand you've overseen this cemetery for many years. Your guidance would be invaluable."

Murphy's eyes fixed on the coin, his professional demeanour warming considerably. "Been here fifteen years, miss. Know every plot and stone."

"Then perhaps you might advise me on recent interments as well? My uncle was particular about his company, even in death." Elizabeth allowed the half-crown to catch the spring sunlight. "Which families have recently laid loved ones to rest here?"

The groundskeeper glanced around before answering, confirming they were alone. "Three burials yesterday. Elderly woman in the north corner, consumption, by the look of her. Young man, twenty or so, south side, drowning victim. And a gentleman of means, east section, heart failure, according to the doctor."

Elizabeth nodded thoughtfully, her mind cataloguing these details according to the system she'd developed over months of such inquiries. The drowning victim would be of particular interest; young specimens in good condition commanded premium prices for anatomy classes.

"And the security arrangements? My uncle valued privacy above all things."

"Night watchman patrols until midnight," Murphy answered, now speaking as one professional to another, their true transaction understood beneath the pretence. "After that, only occasional rounds. East gate lock's been troublesome this past week." He accepted the coin with practised casualness. "Anything else the family should know?"

"That will suffice for now." Elizabeth offered a slight smile. "Though I may return with additional questions as arrangements progress."

As she departed the churchyard, Elizabeth mentally added Murphy to her growing network of informants. Over the past months, she had cultivated relationships throughout London's funeral industry: groundskeepers who provided burial schedules, servants from wealthy households who reported on elderly or sick family members, and even parish clerks who recorded deaths and could be persuaded to share information for modest compensation.

Her refined speech and apparent respectability

allowed her access that Bob's more obvious working-class background could never achieve. Together, they had transformed their initial clumsy operation into a methodical business that generated a steady income far exceeding what legitimate employment might have offered either of them.

The spring air carried the scent of new growth as Elizabeth made her way through streets that had become familiar territory over the past months. Their operation had expanded beyond mere survival to something approaching prosperity, modest but secure. The desperate girl who had fled Veronica's murderous rage had evolved into a calculating businesswoman with a network of contacts across London's death industry.

When she reached their lodgings of two rooms above a chandler's shop in a neighbourhood neither respectable nor truly dangerous, Bob was waiting with tea already brewing. Their accommodations reflected their improved circumstances: simple furniture but clean linens, a small stove for cooking and warmth, and a lock on the door that deterred casual intrusion.

"Murphy proved helpful," Elizabeth reported, removing her bonnet and gloves. "Three fresh burials, including a drowning victim of approximately twenty years. Young, male, no disease; perfect for Dr. Pemberton's anatomy class."

Bob nodded approvingly as he poured the tea. At nineteen, he had grown more confident in his own role within their partnership, his natural intelligence finding expression in the practical aspects of their enterprise.

"Night watchman?" he asked.

"Patrols until midnight, then sporadic. East gate lock is conveniently faulty." Elizabeth accepted the cup he offered. "We should move tonight, before the body begins significant decomposition."

The clinical discussion of their grim business no longer disturbed her as it once had. Necessity had bred familiarity, and familiarity had eventually produced a professional detachment that allowed her to view corpses as commodities rather than desecrated remains. The moral qualms that had overwhelmed her after their first operation still surfaced occasionally but had been largely subsumed by practical considerations of survival and, increasingly, success.

"I've prepared the equipment," Bob said, gesturing toward their specialised tools stored in a locked trunk: shovels designed for quiet, efficient digging; canvas wrappings to muffle the sound of metal against wood; cloths soaked in vinegar to mask the smell of decay when necessary.

Elizabeth nodded, her attention turning to the small desk that served as her business headquarters. There, she maintained detailed records of potential "acquisitions," organised by location, estimated condition, and likely value. Medical journals obtained from second-hand booksellers helped her understand which specimens commanded premium prices, unusual conditions for pathology study, specific age groups for anatomy classes, and particular organs for specialised research.

"Dr. Pemberton mentioned the Royal College is seeking female specimens for obstetrical training," she noted, consulting her records. "We should prioritise those in the coming weeks. The compensation is substantially higher than standard specimens."

"Crowe's gang has been working the Highgate women's section," Bob pointed out. "We'd be encroaching on their territory."

Elizabeth's expression hardened slightly at the mention of Thomas Crowe, whose established resurrection gang dominated the eastern cemetery districts. Their growing operation had already attracted unwelcome attention from Crowe's associates, veiled warnings about respecting territorial boundaries, and demands for tribute that they had thus far ignored.

"We'll focus on the smaller parishes for now," she decided. "Less profitable individually but safer until we're better established."

Their business discussion continued through tea, the macabre subject matter handled with the same practical attention any merchant might give to inventory and market conditions. Only occasionally did Elizabeth catch glimpses of their true circumstances as two young people discussing grave robbery with the seriousness of bankers reviewing investments.

In these moments, she sometimes wondered what her mother would think of the woman she had become. Mary Flanders had chosen comfort over moral courage, remaining with a criminal husband rather than facing poverty. Had Elizabeth's choices been so different? She had embraced the very criminality she once viewed with reluctance, adapting to circumstances with a pragmatism that sometimes frightened her.

Yet there was undeniable satisfaction in their accomplishments: a business built from nothing, and survival secured through intelligence and determination rather than the protection of others. Whatever moral compromises their enterprise required, Elizabeth had discovered capabilities within herself that might otherwise have remained dormant.

And there was Bob, whose presence in her life had evolved from a necessary alliance to something deeper and more complex. Their partnership, born of mutual need, had gradually developed dimensions beyond business, encompassing trust, affection, and increasingly, an unspoken emotional connection that neither had directly acknowledged.

As evening approached and they prepared for the night's operation, Elizabeth found herself watching Bob with a warmth that had nothing to do with their professional relationship. The careful way he checked their equipment, his thoughtful consideration of potential risks, his quiet competence, all had become precious to her in ways she hadn't anticipated when they'd first formed their partnership.

"Ready?" he asked, catching her gaze.

Elizabeth nodded, pushing personal reflections aside to focus on the work ahead. Tonight they would secure another specimen, sell it to Dr. Pemberton tomorrow, and add the proceeds to their growing savings. One operation at a time, they were building security from the most unlikely of foundations.

* * *

"THE SPECIMEN EXHIBITS PRECISELY the conditions your students require for understanding pulmonary structures," Elizabeth explained, her tone professionally detached as she stood in Dr. Pemberton's private office at St. Bartholomew's Hospital. "Male, approximately twenty years of age, excellent musculature, and the drowning provides ideal visualisation of the lung tissue in its natural state."

Dr. Pemberton nodded appreciatively, adjusting his spectacles as he examined the documentation Elizabeth had provided as her own creation, a system of notes that detailed the specimen's characteristics without revealing its source. The actual body waited in an anteroom, delivered earlier through the hospital's discreet receiving entrance where such transactions occurred away from public view.

"Most impressive, Miss Smith," he replied, using the professional alias Elizabeth had adopted for their business dealings. "Your attention to our specific requirements distinguishes your services from other suppliers."

Elizabeth accepted the compliment with a slight inclination of her head. Over the past months, their reputation for reliability and quality had earned them regular business from St. Bartholomew's and, increasingly, other medical institutions seeking specimens for research and education.

"The Royal College mentioned your operation favourably," Dr. Pemberton continued, reaching for his cashbox. "Quite remarkable for newcomers to establish such a reputation so quickly."

"We prioritise quality and discretion," Elizabeth replied, watching as he counted out eight pounds—a premium price reflecting the specimen's exceptional condition. "Medical education requires the finest materials."

The rationalisation came easily now, her father's justification for grave robbing adopted as her own. By providing bodies for anatomical study, they contributed to the training of surgeons and physicians who would save countless lives. The moral calculus might be questionable, but the practical benefit was real, both to medical science and to Elizabeth and Bob's continued survival.

When she departed St. Bartholomew's with

payment secured in her reticule, Elizabeth reflected on their progress since that first nervous transaction months ago. Then, they had been desperate novices, grateful for any payment. Now, they approached medical institutions with confidence, negotiating favourable terms and developing ongoing relationships with key personnel.

The spring afternoon was pleasant, London's perpetual coal smoke temporarily dispersed by a brisk breeze. Elizabeth walked with the measured pace of a respectable young woman on legitimate business, her dark blue dress modest but well-maintained, her demeanour giving no hint of her nocturnal activities or criminal connections.

She had learned to navigate multiple worlds with chameleon-like adaptability, speaking the refined language of medical professionals in morning negotiations, then shifting to the practical terminology of the resurrection trade when planning operations with Bob, and adopting yet another persona when gathering information from servants and cemetery workers.

This ability to cross social boundaries proved invaluable to their enterprise. Elizabeth's education allowed her to understand medical requirements and negotiate with physicians, while her observations of her father's business provided insights into the organisational aspects of their trade. Bob contributed practical knowledge of London's geography, street survival skills, and the physical aspects of their work.

Together, they had created something neither could have managed alone: a resurrection business sophisticated enough to command respect from established medical institutions yet small enough to avoid the worst attention from competing gangs or authorities.

Elizabeth turned down a side street, her path taking her through progressively less genteel neighbourhoods as she approached their lodgings. The transition felt symbolic of her own journey from respectable merchant's daughter to grave robber's accomplice to criminal entrepreneur in her own right.

She was crossing a small market square when she noticed a familiar figure leaning against a building ahead. Jenkins, one of Thomas Crowe's known associates. His posture appeared casual, but his gaze tracked her with predatory focus that sent a warning prickle along her spine.

Elizabeth maintained her pace, neither hurrying nor showing obvious concern. When their paths inevitably converged, Jenkins straightened, blocking her way with deliberate insolence.

"Miss Smith," he said, using her professional alias with a sneer that suggested he knew it was false. "Mr. Crowe sends his compliments."

"How thoughtful," Elizabeth replied coolly. "Please convey my regards in return."

Jenkins' smile didn't reach his eyes. "Mr. Crowe also sends a message. Your activities in the eastern parishes have been noted. Those are established territories with existing arrangements."

"I wasn't aware that cemetery grounds required permission beyond the official authorities," Elizabeth said, her tone deliberately naive while her mind calculated potential escape routes should this encounter turn violent.

"Don't play innocent, girl. You know how this works." Jenkins leaned closer, his voice lowering. "Ten per cent of your takings for operations in the eastern districts, or find somewhere else to dig. That's generous; Crowe usually demands twenty."

Elizabeth met his gaze steadily, showing neither fear nor defiance. "I'll consider Mr. Crowe's proposal and discuss it with my associate."

"Don't consider too long," Jenkins warned. "Next message won't be delivered with words." He stepped aside, allowing her to pass. "Crowe knows where you live. Above the chandler's, ain't it? Cosy little setup."

The implied threat chilled Elizabeth despite the spring warmth, but she kept her expression neutral as she continued past him. The knowledge that Crowe's gang had identified their lodgings represented a significant escalation from general awareness of their operation to specific intelligence that could lead to direct confrontation.

When she reached their rooms, she found Bob at the table cleaning their tools after the previous night's work. His expression shifted instantly upon seeing her face.

"What happened?" he asked, setting aside the cloth he'd been using.

Elizabeth recounted her encounter with Jenkins, including the demand for payment and the veiled threat. While she spoke, she removed her bonnet and gloves, transforming from respectable Miss Smith back to Elizabeth Flanders, resurrectionist and businesswoman.

"We knew this would come eventually," Bob said when she finished. "Crowe doesn't tolerate independent operators in what he considers his territory."

"We've been careful to avoid his primary hunting

grounds," Elizabeth pointed out, placing the payment from Dr. Pemberton in their hidden cash-box. "But the eastern parishes have the freshest burials this month."

"Ten per cent is actually reasonable," Bob mused. "Most small operations pay more for Crowe's 'protection.'"

Elizabeth's eyes narrowed thoughtfully. "Which suggests he views us as worth cultivating rather than eliminating outright. Interesting."

Bob studied her with a mixture of admiration and concern. "You're thinking like a criminal, Lizzie."

"I am a criminal," she replied simply. "We both are. Might as well think like one."

The frank acknowledgement hung between them, neither uncomfortable nor proud, simply factual. Their circumstances had pushed them into criminality, but their success within that world had come from embracing its realities rather than maintaining illusions about their choices.

"We should consider relocating," Bob suggested. "If Crowe knows where we live—"

"No," Elizabeth interrupted, a strategy already forming in her mind. "Moving shows weakness and fear. Instead, we'll pay his ten per cent on eastern parish operations while expanding elsewhere." She began pacing, her thoughts racing ahead. "The western cemeteries are controlled by smaller gangs with whom we could potentially negotiate directly. The southern parishes are practically untouched due to poorer security but lower-value burials."

Bob watched her with growing amazement as she outlined a comprehensive territorial strategy that would allow them to maintain profitability while managing the threat from Crowe's organisation.

"You've become quite the strategist," he observed when she finally paused.

Elizabeth stopped her pacing, suddenly self-conscious under his gaze. "My father taught me to analyse business challenges systematically. This is just... an unusual application of those lessons."

"Your father would be proud," Bob said, then immediately regretted his words as Elizabeth's expression clouded.

"Yes," she agreed quietly. "He would be. That's what disturbs me sometimes."

Bob rose from the table, crossing to where she stood. With uncharacteristic boldness, he took her hand in his. "You're not him, Elizabeth. You didn't choose this life, it was forced upon you."

"Was it?" she questioned, not withdrawing her

hand but looking at him with genuine uncertainty. "We could have begged. Or I could have sought factory work. There were other paths, however difficult."

"None that would have preserved what makes you who you are," Bob insisted. "Your intelligence, your dignity, your independence."

Elizabeth smiled faintly at his defence of her choices. "Perhaps. Or perhaps I discovered I have more of my father in me than I ever wanted to acknowledge."

The conversation might have continued in this philosophical vein, but practical concerns intervened. They needed to prepare for that night's operation, a wealthy widow's burial in a parish cemetery that fell just outside Crowe's claimed territory. The moral implications of their work could be examined another time.

As they gathered their equipment and reviewed the cemetery layout, Elizabeth found comfort in the familiar routine they had established over months of working together. Bob's presence beside her had become essential to her sense of security in ways that transcended their business partnership.

When had that happened? When had this young man, once a stranger who grabbed her arm, suspecting her of pickpocketing, become someone whose approval mattered, whose safety concerned her more than her own, whose rare smiles could brighten even the darkest aspects of their shared enterprise?

Elizabeth pushed these questions aside, focusing instead on the practical details of the night ahead. Emotions were a luxury they could ill afford when survival remained their primary concern.

* * *

Over the following weeks, Elizabeth implemented her strategy for managing Crowe's demands while expanding their operation in other directions. They paid the required percentage on eastern parish operations but gradually shifted their focus to territories where Crowe's influence was weaker.

Elizabeth also began a systematic study of Crowe's organisation itself, gathering intelligence through their network of informants. She created detailed files on his methods, associates, and weaknesses; knowledge that might prove valuable should their uneasy arrangement deteriorate into open conflict.

Their business continued to thrive despite these

complications. Dr. Pemberton introduced Elizabeth to colleagues at other medical institutions, expanding their customer base beyond St. Bartholomew's. Their reputation for providing quality specimens meeting specific research needs commanded premium prices that more than offset Crowe's percentage demands.

With increased income came modest improvements to their living situation. Elizabeth purchased better clothing for her negotiations with medical professionals. Bob acquired additional equipment that made their nocturnal work more efficient and less physically demanding. Their lodgings remained simple but now contained small comforts like better food, warmer blankets, and a few books for evening reading.

One night in late spring, returning from a successful operation in a small parish cemetery, Elizabeth caught sight of her reflection in a shop window. The image startled her, not because it showed anything unusual, but because she momentarily failed to recognise herself.

The young woman looking back bore little resemblance to the frightened girl who had fled Veronica's murderous rage less than a year earlier. This Elizabeth stood straighter, moved with quiet confidence, and carried herself with the self-possession of someone who had faced extreme challenges and survived through her own resources.

Elizabeth studied this stranger who was herself, noting the changes that went beyond physical appearance. Her expression held a calculation that hadn't existed before, her eyes assessing her surroundings with the automatic vigilance of someone accustomed to operating outside the law. Even her posture reflected her transformation, no longer the proper stance of a merchant's daughter but the balanced readiness of a woman who might need to run or fight at any moment.

"Something wrong?" Bob asked, noticing her preoccupation with the reflection.

"Just thinking about how much has changed," Elizabeth replied, resuming their walk toward home. "Sometimes I hardly recognise myself."

Bob considered this as they navigated the quiet streets, their package, tonight's "specimen", secured in a specially designed carrying case that resembled ordinary luggage.

"People adapt to their circumstances," he said finally. "You've done what was necessary to survive."

"It's more than survival now, though," Elizabeth admitted. "I take pride in what we've built. I enjoy the challenge of outwitting competitors, negotiating better prices, and developing new contacts." She glanced at him uncertainly. "What does that say about me?"

Bob's response was thoughtful rather than immediately reassuring. "It says you're intelligent and resourceful. That you've found a way to thrive in circumstances that would destroy most people."

"My father said something similar once, justifying his own choices." Elizabeth's voice held no judgment, merely observation. "He claimed he was simply using his talents in the only field open to him after some early business failures."

They walked in silence for several moments, the comparison to William Flanders hanging between them. Finally, Bob spoke again.

"There's a difference between your father and you," he said quietly. "He chose his path from several options, then dragged his family into danger. You were forced onto your path by others' actions, then created something that protected both of us."

The distinction offered some comfort, though Elizabeth wasn't entirely convinced. Had necessity truly dictated all her choices, or had she discovered an affinity for this shadowy business that existed independently of circumstance?

When they reached their lodgings and secured their acquisition for tomorrow's delivery, Elizabeth found herself watching Bob as he moved about their rooms, preparing tea before they slept. His presence had become essential to her in ways that transcended their business partnership; a constancy she had never expected to find in the chaos following her flight from Veronica.

"Bob," she said impulsively, "are you ever sorry you helped me that day in the market?"

He looked up, genuine surprise crossing his features. "Sorry? For finding the best business partner and friend I could have imagined?" He shook his head, a rare smile softening his usually serious expression. "Not for a moment."

The simple sincerity of his answer warmed Elizabeth more than the tea he handed her. Whatever moral ambiguities clouded their enterprise, whatever dangers they faced from Crowe's gang or authorities, this connection between them remained untainted; a partnership that had evolved into genuine affection neither had anticipated.

As they discussed the next day's delivery and future operations, Elizabeth acknowledged to herself what she had been reluctant to examine directly: she had built something substantial from nothing, a business that provided not just survival but a measure of security and even modest prosperity.

That this business involved grave robbery and operated outside the law didn't diminish the achievement, though it certainly complicated her feelings about it. She had discovered capabilities within herself: organisational skills, strategic thinking, and negotiation tactics that might have remained dormant in the protected environment of her former life.

The girl who had once viewed her father's criminal activities with reluctance and moral qualms had become a woman who applied those same methods with increasing confidence and skill. The transformation disturbed her in moments of reflection, but also filled her with a complicated pride. She had not merely survived, she had adapted and thrived in circumstances that should have destroyed her.

Later, preparing for bed in the small alcove that served as her private space, Elizabeth caught sight of her reflection again in the small mirror above her washbasin. The face that looked back was neither the innocent child she had been nor the hardened criminal she sometimes feared becoming, but something more complex: a young woman shaped by difficult choices and harsh realities, yet still capable of warmth, loyalty, and moral questioning.

Whether this transformation represented growth or corruption remained an open question. Elizabeth had become someone her mother would scarcely recognise, and her father would ironically approve of. A young woman who had taken his criminal legacy and adapted it to her own survival with intelligence and determination.

As she extinguished her candle and settled beneath her blankets, Elizabeth acknowledged the central paradox of her current life: the very circumstances that had nearly destroyed her had also revealed strengths she might never have discovered otherwise. The resurrection trade that had once represented everything she wished to avoid had become the foundation of her independence and security.

Tomorrow would bring new challenges: Crowe's territorial demands, medical schools' specific requirements, and the constant vigilance needed to avoid authorities. But it would also bring another day of applying her intelligence to problems she was increasingly equipped to solve, another opportunity to build upon the unexpected partnership with Bob that had become precious to her.

Elizabeth closed her eyes, her mind already planning tomorrow's negotiation with Dr. Pemberton's colleague at Guy's Hospital. She had built something substantial from nothing, using the only resources available to her, knowledge of her father's criminal business and her own adaptable intelligence.

Whether the cost of that achievement would eventually prove too high in moral compromise, in danger, in the hardening of her character, remained to be seen. For now, she had transformed from victim to survivor to entrepreneur through sheer determination and an unexpected partnership.

That transformation, with all its moral complexity, was something she had earned through her own efforts in a world that offered few options to a young woman alone. Whatever judgment might eventually fall upon her choices, Elizabeth had claimed her place in London's shadowy underworld not merely as William Flanders' daughter but as a resurrection woman in her own right.

CHAPTER 10

The same face appeared again, third time this week. Elizabeth pretended to examine fabric at a market stall while watching the reflection in a nearby shop window. A rough-looking man with a pockmarked face and broad shoulders, too well-dressed for this neighbourhood but trying to blend in. He maintained a careful distance, but his eyes never left her.

Not one of Crowe's men, they made no effort to hide their surveillance, wanting her to know she was being watched. This was something different. Something worse.

Elizabeth selected a length of dark blue cotton, paid the vendor, and moved deeper into the market's crowded lanes. A practised turn at a baker's stall, a swift duck behind a pile of crates, and she emerged into a narrow alley that offered a clear view of the main thoroughfare.

The man appeared moments later, scanning the crowd with obvious frustration. His movements betrayed professional training: methodical, patient, eyes constantly sweeping possible hiding places. He wasn't a common thug, but someone accustomed to hunting human prey.

Elizabeth pressed herself against the damp brick wall as he passed the alley entrance. This was the third such man she'd noticed in recent weeks, all watching her operations sites and lodgings with the same calculating attention.

"Looking for someone?"

The whispered question made Elizabeth whirl around, knife already half-drawn before she recognised Murphy, the cemetery groundskeeper who provided information about fresh burials.

"You startled me," she said, returning the blade to its hidden sheath.

"Better me than him." Murphy nodded toward the street where the man continued his search. "You've got trouble, miss. People have been asking questions about you all over. Describing a well-spoken girl who buys information about burials."

"Crowe's men?"

Murphy shook his head. "Different sort. These ones have money to spend. Offering rewards for information on your whereabouts." He glanced nervously toward the street. "Thought you should know. I ain't told them nothing, but others might not be so loyal."

Elizabeth pressed a coin into his palm. "Thank you, Murphy. You've done me a great service."

After he departed, Elizabeth remained in the alley, her mind racing. The description, the professional quality of the surveillance, the offered rewards; this wasn't Thomas Crowe expanding his intimidation campaign. This was Veronica, still hunting for the stepdaughter who had escaped her murderous intentions.

For months, Elizabeth had focused entirely on building their resurrection business and managing Crowe's territorial threats. She'd allowed herself to believe Veronica might have abandoned the search after so much time had passed. That comfortable illusion now shattered like glass beneath a hammer blow.

She needed to warn Bob to change their routines immediately. If Veronica's hunters had identified her, they would soon trace her to their lodgings.

Everything they'd built stood in immediate jeopardy.

Elizabeth waited until certain the man had moved on, then took a circuitous route back toward their rooms, checking frequently for followers and changing direction multiple times. The sense of being prey had returned with visceral intensity, reminding her of those first desperate days after fleeing Veronica's house.

But she was no longer that frightened girl. Months of operating in London's criminal underworld had taught her observation skills, strategic thinking, and most importantly, that knowledge was power. If Veronica was hunting her, Elizabeth needed to understand exactly what she faced.

That meant watching the hunter herself.

* * *

THE TOWNHOUSE LOOKED EXACTLY as Elizabeth remembered, a respectable façade concealing darker activities within. From her vantage point across the street, partially hidden by a greengrocer's awning, she observed the home that had once been hers, now fully under Veronica's control.

Patience yielded results near midday when the

front door opened, and Veronica emerged. At nineteen, her beauty had only intensified with her violet eyes bright with intelligence, dark hair arranged fashionably beneath an expensive bonnet, and her figure shown to advantage in a walking dress of deep burgundy. No one seeing this elegant young widow would imagine the calculated evil behind that perfect exterior.

Elizabeth followed at a safe distance as Veronica made her way through London's fashionable districts, eventually stopping at a handsome residence in Belgravia. A servant admitted her immediately, with the deference shown to an expected and welcome visitor.

Positioning herself in a small park opposite, Elizabeth settled on a bench with a borrowed book, the perfect prop for extended observation. Two hours passed before Veronica emerged, now accompanied by an elderly woman leaning heavily on her arm. Their body language told the story clearly: Veronica solicitous and attentive, the older woman grateful for the support of her charming young friend.

Even at this distance, Elizabeth recognised the familiar pattern. Veronica had identified another target: wealthy, isolated, and vulnerable to the particular brand of attentive friendship that preceded her systematic poisoning.

When they parted at the street corner, Veronica's mask slipped momentarily. The warm smile disappeared, replaced by the cold calculation Elizabeth remembered all too well. She consulted a small notebook before tucking it into her reticule, her expression one of professional satisfaction rather than friendly concern.

Elizabeth followed the elderly woman instead of Veronica, needing to confirm her suspicions. The neighbourhood's affluence, the quality of the woman's clothing, and the deference shown by shopkeepers all suggested substantial wealth. A discreet inquiry at a nearby bakery yielded the information she sought.

"That's Mrs. Catherine Hartwell," the baker's wife informed her. "Widow these past five years. No children, keeps to herself mostly, though she's been seen about more lately with that lovely young companion."

"They seem quite close," Elizabeth observed.

"Been a blessing for the old lady, that one has. Visits daily with special teas and remedies. Such a thoughtful friend to someone so alone." The woman leaned closer. "Though Mrs. Hartwell's health has been delicate these past weeks. Stomach troubles, poor thing."

Elizabeth's chest tightened. Stomach troubles, the first sign of Veronica's poisoning regimen, just as her mother had experienced. The pattern was unmistakable, the methodology unchanged despite Veronica's greater wealth and social position.

Her murder business had become more sophisticated and profitable than William's grave robbing ever was. While Elizabeth and Bob struggled to build their modest resurrection enterprise, Veronica had perfected her approach to eliminating wealthy widows and inheriting their assets.

The irony wasn't lost on Elizabeth that both she and her stepmother had constructed criminal careers from death, though through different methods and motivations. Veronica killed for profit and perhaps pleasure; Elizabeth merely exploited those already deceased, out of necessity rather than choice.

The moral distinction offered cold comfort as she made her way back toward their lodgings. Veronica's hunters represented a threat greater than Crowe's territorial intimidation. If found, Elizabeth wouldn't face mere business competition but certain death at the hands of a woman who eliminated obstacles with methodical precision.

She needed to warn Bob immediately and implement new security measures. Their survival depended on disappearing from Veronica's hunters while maintaining enough of their operation to support themselves.

* * *

Elizabeth knew something was wrong before she reached their door. The hallway was too quiet, the familiar sounds of other lodgers absent. The door itself stood slightly ajar; they never left it unlocked, let alone open.

She approached cautiously, every sense alert for danger. Through the narrow opening, she glimpsed their room in disarray with furniture overturned, their carefully organised business records scattered across the floor, and the mattress slashed open with feathers drifting in the still air.

Someone had thoroughly ransacked their lodgings, searching for something or waiting for someone.

Elizabeth backed away silently, intending to find Bob before attempting to enter, when a floorboard creaked beneath her foot. The door swung open immediately, revealing a large man with a scar across his left cheek.

"There you are," he said with grim satisfaction. "Been waiting a while, Miss Flanders."

Elizabeth turned to flee, but another man appeared at the stairwell behind her, blocking her escape. Veronica's hunters had found them.

"Come in quiet-like," the scarred man said, gesturing with a hand that bore the calluses of someone accustomed to violence. "We just want a conversation."

Elizabeth knew better. Men like these weren't paid for conversations. She assessed her options with the rapid calculation born of months living on society's margins. Two against one, in a confined space, with no witnesses likely to intervene.

"Where's my partner?" she asked, playing for time while her hand moved slowly toward the knife concealed in her skirt pocket.

"Not here," the second man replied. "Makes things simpler."

They were lying. Bob would never leave their rooms unlocked. Which meant he was either gone or inside and unable to respond.

Elizabeth allowed herself to be herded into the

room, maintaining the appearance of compliance while cataloguing potential weapons and escape routes. The destruction was worse than she'd glimpsed from outside, with everything of value taken or broken, and their carefully built life reduced to splinters and torn paper.

A slight movement behind the overturned table caught her attention. Bob's boot, visible for just an instant before disappearing from view. He was here, conscious, and choosing to remain hidden. A strategic advantage, if she could create the right opportunity.

"Mrs. Flanders wants a word with her stepdaughter," the scarred man said, closing the door behind them. "Been looking for you a long time."

"I'm sure she has," Elizabeth replied, her voice steadier than she felt. "Though I doubt conversation is her primary interest."

"Smart girl." The man's smile revealed tobacco-stained teeth. "Makes no difference to us. We get paid either way: finding you or bringing you back."

Elizabeth's hand closed around her knife handle. "And if I decline the invitation?"

"Then we bring back whatever's left," the second man said, producing a heavy cudgel from his coat. "Your choice how difficult this gets."

Elizabeth had survived on London's streets too long to harbour illusions about mercy from such men. They would beat her unconscious, drag her to Veronica, and collect their payment without hesitation or remorse.

She drew her knife in one fluid motion, the blade catching light from the window. "I'm not going anywhere."

The men exchanged glances, momentarily surprised by her resistance but not particularly concerned. They had faced armed opponents before and clearly considered a young woman with a small knife little threat.

"Hard way, then," the scarred man sighed, reaching inside his coat.

Before he could withdraw whatever weapon he carried, Bob erupted from behind the overturned table, launching himself at the second man with the focused violence of someone who had fought for survival since childhood. They crashed into the wall, Bob's fist connecting with brutal efficiency against the man's throat.

Elizabeth seized the momentary distraction, slashing at the scarred man's outstretched arm. The blade opened a red line across his forearm, causing him to curse and recoil. She followed with a swift kick to his knee, a street-fighting technique Bob had taught her for dealing with larger opponents.

The room dissolved into chaos, furniture splintering, bodies colliding in the confined space, and the grunts and impacts of desperate combat. Bob fought with the ruthless pragmatism of London's streets, targeting vulnerable points without hesitation. Elizabeth employed speed and precision against the scarred man's superior strength, keeping her blade in constant motion to prevent him closing the distance.

A shocking impact against her ribs sent Elizabeth stumbling backwards, breath driven from her lungs by the scarred man's fist. He pressed his advantage, grabbing her knife wrist and twisting until pain forced her fingers open. The knife clattered to the floor as he drove her against the wall, his scarred face inches from hers.

"Should've come quiet," he growled, raising his fist for a blow that would likely render her unconscious.

Elizabeth drove her knee upward with all her strength, striking the most vulnerable target available. The man's grip loosened as he doubled over, allowing her to slip free and retrieve her fallen knife.

Across the room, Bob had pinned the second

man to the floor, blood streaming from the man's nose as Bob delivered another punishing blow. The fight had turned in their favour, but Elizabeth knew it could reverse just as quickly.

"Bob! We need to go!"

He looked up, his expression momentarily unfamiliar, harder and more violent than she had ever seen. Then recognition returned, and he delivered a final blow that left his opponent motionless before scrambling to his feet.

"Back door," he gasped, blood trickling from a cut above his eye.

They fled through the service entrance as shouts rose from the front of the building. Their carefully constructed life lay in ruins behind them, but they had escaped with what mattered most, their lives and each other.

Six streets and numerous turns later, certain they weren't being followed, they paused in the shelter of a church portico to assess injuries and options.

"Are you hurt?" Bob asked, examining Elizabeth with concern.

"Bruised ribs, nothing broken." She winced as she probed her side. "You're bleeding."

"Scalp wound. Looks worse than it is." He wiped blood from his eye. "They were waiting when I returned. Caught me from behind, but I played unconscious until I could see an opening."

Elizabeth leaned against the stone column, the adrenaline of combat fading into the cold reality of their situation. "They found us. Everything we built—"

"Things can be replaced," Bob interrupted firmly. "You can't."

The simple declaration warmed Elizabeth despite their circumstances. In the chaos of flight and fighting, one certainty remained: they faced these dangers together.

"We need a new safe location," she said, forcing her mind back to practical matters. "And to understand exactly what we're facing."

Bob nodded grimly. "Veronica's hunters are one problem. But this feels like more than that."

"Crowe," Elizabeth agreed. "The timing's too convenient. I think Veronica's men found us through Crowe's surveillance."

"Two enemies working together?"

"Not intentionally. But Crowe's men have been watching us for weeks. Veronica's hunters likely observed them to find our location." Elizabeth straightened despite the pain in her ribs. "We need to move quickly. Establish a new base before either group realises we've escaped."

After they slipped back into London's crowded streets, Elizabeth's mind raced with implications and strategies. Their resurrection business faced threats from two directions now: Crowe's territorial aggression and Veronica's deadly hunt. Surviving would require more than simply relocating; they needed to understand their enemies better than their enemies understood them.

And while Bob gathered their emergency funds from a hiding place known only to them, Elizabeth made a decision that surprised even herself. She would not merely hide from Veronica, she would actively counter her former stepmother's murderous plans.

Starting with saving Catherine Hartwell's life.

* * *

Elizabeth watched Mrs. Hartwell's residence from across the street, noting the drawn curtains and the doctor's carriage parked outside. After three days of careful observation, she had confirmed her worst fears, that the elderly widow was already well into Veronica's poisoning regimen, showing the same symptoms Mary Flanders had exhibited before her death.

When the doctor emerged, his expression told the story clearly: professional concern masking confusion about a condition he couldn't properly diagnose. Elizabeth had seen that same look on Dr. Morrison's face during her mother's final illness.

She followed the physician to his next appointment, gathering her courage before approaching him as he returned to his carriage.

"Excuse me, Doctor," she called, adopting her most respectable manner. "Might I inquire about Mrs. Hartwell's condition? I'm from her church, and we've been most concerned."

The grey-haired man studied her briefly before responding. "Mrs. Hartwell is experiencing some digestive disturbances. Nothing immediately alarming, though her weakness concerns me."

"Has she been taking any special remedies? Herbal preparations, perhaps?"

The doctor's eyebrows rose slightly. "As a matter of fact, yes. A young friend has been preparing tonics that Mrs. Hartwell finds quite soothing. Miss Ashworth, I believe." He tilted his head curiously. "Do you know her?"

"By reputation," Elizabeth replied carefully.

"These tonics, they provide temporary relief followed by worsening symptoms?"

"How did you know that?" The doctor's professional interest was clearly piqued.

"I've observed similar cases," Elizabeth said, which was true enough. "Doctor, I believe Mrs. Hartwell would benefit from discontinuing these preparations immediately."

"That's rather presumptuous advice from a church acquaintance," he noted, though without dismissing her entirely.

"Perhaps. But I would strongly suggest having Mrs. Hartwell monitored by someone other than Miss Ashworth for the next several days. If her condition improves without the tonics, you'll have valuable diagnostic information."

The doctor studied her more carefully. "You seem unusually knowledgeable for a young woman from the church committee."

"I have a particular interest in certain types of poisoning," Elizabeth replied, meeting his gaze directly. "Especially those that mimic natural illness."

Understanding dawned in the doctor's eyes. "That's a serious implication."

"One worth investigating, given Mrs. Hartwell's wealth and isolation," Elizabeth countered. "Particularly if Miss Ashworth stands to benefit from her passing."

She could see the physician reassessing the situation, medical training overcoming his initial scepticism. "I'll look into the matter," he said finally. "Though I hope you realise the gravity of such accusations."

"I do, Doctor. More than you know."

As he departed, Elizabeth knew her intervention might not be sufficient. The doctor might dismiss her concerns, or Veronica's influence over Mrs. Hartwell might be too strong to overcome through third-party warnings.

A more direct approach was needed.

That evening, Elizabeth composed a letter in carefully disguised handwriting, detailing Veronica's methodology and previous victims, including Mary Flanders. She provided specific information about the poisoning symptoms and suggested immediate measures to confirm her accusations, including having all food and drink tested, dismissing Veronica from the household, and consulting additional physicians.

She delivered the letter personally, slipping it under Mrs. Hartwell's door after confirming Veronica had departed for the evening. Whether the widow would believe an anonymous warning remained uncertain, but Elizabeth had done what she could without exposing herself directly.

The moral calculus was complex. Warning Mrs. Hartwell risked drawing attention that might lead Veronica's hunters back to Elizabeth. Yet allowing another murder when she possessed the knowledge to prevent it seemed unconscionable, regardless of her own criminal activities.

Elizabeth had crossed many lines since fleeing Veronica's house, but she would not cross this one. Whatever she had become, resurrection woman, grave robber, criminal, she would not be complicit in murder through inaction.

As she made her way back to the abandoned workshop where she and Bob had established temporary shelter, Elizabeth considered the potential consequences of her intervention. If successful, she would save a life but also enrage Veronica. The hunt would intensify; the danger would increase.

But for the first time since discovering Veronica's hunters, Elizabeth felt something beyond fear: a sense of purpose and moral clarity that had been absent in their resurrection business. Stopping Veronica's murder of Mrs. Hartwell wouldn't erase Elizabeth's own criminal choices, but it represented a line she refused to cross, a boundary between types of wrongdoing she still distinguished between.

Bob was waiting with news of his own when she returned to their makeshift lodgings.

"Murphy was attacked today," he reported grimly. "Crowe's men caught him leaving the Southwark cemetery. Beat him badly enough to send a message but not enough to kill him."

"Because of his connection to us?"

Bob nodded. "A warning to our other informants. Crowe's escalating his campaign."

Elizabeth absorbed this development, adding it to her mental map of the threats surrounding them. "We need to move our operations entirely. New territories, new informants, new medical school contacts."

"That means rebuilding everything," Bob pointed out. "Months of work lost."

"Not lost but transformed." Elizabeth's mind was already racing ahead, seeing opportunity within catastrophe. "We know the business now, understand its weaknesses. We can construct something more resilient."

Bob studied her with a mixture of admiration and concern. "You're not thinking of giving up, are you? Even with Veronica hunting you?"

"Giving up would mean surrendering to her," Elizabeth replied, her voice hardening. "I won't do that. Not after everything we've built."

The determination in her tone seemed to reassure him. They spent the evening planning their next steps, new cemetery targets beyond Crowe's territory, potential safe locations for more permanent lodgings, and alternative medical contacts beyond their established relationships.

Three days later, Elizabeth's intervention bore unexpected fruit. Passing near Mrs. Hartwell's residence during her daily reconnaissance, she witnessed a police constable escorting Veronica from the house. The young woman's perfect composure had cracked, her beautiful face twisted with thwarted rage as she was firmly but respectfully removed from the premises.

From a nearby shopkeeper, Elizabeth learned that Mrs. Hartwell had fallen seriously ill after consuming tea prepared by her young friend. Suspicious after receiving an anonymous letter, she had pretended to drink the preparation while actually preserving it for testing. The results had been sufficiently alarming to involve authorities, although whether charges would be filed remained uncertain given Mrs. Hartwell's reluctance to create a public scandal.

Watching from a safe distance as Veronica departed in a hansom cab, Elizabeth felt a complex mixture of satisfaction and apprehension. She had successfully prevented a murder, but in doing so, had revealed her continued existence to her most dangerous enemy.

That evening, Elizabeth observed Veronica's house from a carefully chosen vantage point, needing to understand how her intervention had affected her stepmother's plans. The increased activity confirmed her worst fears with men coming and going at unusual hours, hushed conversations on the doorstep, and money changing hands.

Veronica was hiring more hunters, offering larger rewards, and expanding her search. The thwarted murder of Mrs. Hartwell had transformed her campaign from methodical elimination of a potential witness into something more personal and vindictive.

Elizabeth retreated to their temporary shelter, her mind working through implications and countermeasures. When she explained what she had observed, Bob's expression grew grave.

"She won't stop now," he said. "Not after you've actively interfered with her plans."

"No," Elizabeth agreed. "This has become something beyond practical concerns for her. My continued existence represents defiance she can't tolerate."

"We should leave London," Bob suggested. "Start fresh somewhere she can't find us."

Elizabeth considered the proposal seriously. Abandoning London meant sacrificing their knowledge of local cemeteries, medical schools, and informant networks. Yet remaining meant facing escalating danger from both Veronica and Crowe.

"Not yet," she decided finally. "Running now would leave us vulnerable, without resources or connections. We need to stabilise our position first, build enough capital to establish ourselves elsewhere if necessary."

Bob accepted her decision without argument, though concern remained evident in his expression. "We'll need better security, new methods for conducting business."

"And better intelligence about our enemies," Elizabeth added. "I've been reactive too long. It's time to understand exactly what we're facing."

While they discussed practical adjustments to

their resurrection business, Elizabeth recognised a fundamental shift in her approach to their situation. She was no longer merely evading Veronica's hunters; she was actively gathering information, analysing vulnerabilities, and planning countermeasures.

The hunted had begun thinking like a hunter.

Later that night, unable to sleep on their makeshift bedding, Elizabeth found herself contemplating the strange symmetry of her conflict with Veronica. Both had constructed lives around death, Elizabeth through resurrection, Veronica through murder. Both operated outside society's laws, using intelligence and methodical planning to achieve their aims.

The crucial difference lay in purpose and method. Veronica killed the living for profit and perhaps pleasure; Elizabeth merely exploited those already deceased, out of necessity rather than choice. The distinction might seem academic to authorities who would condemn them both, but to Elizabeth, it represented an essential moral boundary.

She would not become like Veronica, regardless of what other lines she crossed to survive. Saving Mrs. Hartwell had affirmed that commitment, even at cost to her own safety.

As dawn light filtered through the workshop's grimy windows, Elizabeth made a decision that would alter the nature of their conflict. This war would end only with one of their deaths—Veronica's pathological need to dominate and destroy would accept nothing less. Therefore, Elizabeth's survival depended not just on hiding but on eventually confronting her stepmother directly.

She would continue their resurrection business, rebuilding what Crowe and Veronica had damaged. But alongside that work, she would begin planning her own campaign against the woman who had destroyed her family and murdered her mother.

The predator who had hunted her would discover that prey can develop teeth and claws of their own. Elizabeth had learned much about death's business since fleeing into London's night. Those lessons would now serve a purpose beyond mere survival; they would become weapons in a battle Veronica never expected to fight.

CHAPTER 11

The public house reeked of stale beer and unwashed bodies, its dim interior offering the perfect anonymity for Elizabeth's meeting with Jenkins, a gravedigger from St. Mary's Cemetery who had provided reliable information over the past three months. She sat in the darkest corner, nursing a half-pint of watery ale she had no intention of drinking, watching the door with the habitual vigilance that had become second nature.

Jenkins arrived twenty minutes late, his usual swagger replaced by nervous glances over his shoulder. He slid onto the bench opposite Elizabeth without greeting, his fingers drumming an anxious rhythm on the scarred wooden table.

"This needs to be quick," he muttered, refusing the drink Elizabeth offered. "Shouldn't be seen with you at all."

"What's happened?" Elizabeth kept her voice low, noting the yellowing bruise along Jenkins' jawline partially hidden by several days' stubble.

"Perkins and Wilson were done over proper last night. Broken fingers, cracked ribs." Jenkins leaned closer, dropping his voice further. "Whitby caught it worst, they took his right eye. Said it was for selling information to 'the girl and her boy.'"

Elizabeth's stomach tightened. Perkins, Wilson, and Whitby were all cemetery workers who had provided burial information that was the lifeblood of their resurrection business. Three informants attacked in a single night represented not random violence but coordinated intimidation.

"Crowe's men?"

Jenkins nodded, eyes darting toward the door again. "Had a message for you, too. Said anyone caught working with you gets the same or worse. They're watching all the usual meeting places."

"Yet you came anyway," Elizabeth observed.

"You've been fair with me." Jenkins shrugged uncomfortably. "Figured you deserved warning. But this is the last time; got a wife and little ones. Can't risk ending up like Whitby."

Elizabeth slid a folded banknote across the table as payment for information he hadn't provided, but compensation for his risk nonetheless. "I understand. Keep your head down, Jenkins."

He pocketed the money and departed without another word, leaving Elizabeth alone with the implications of his warning. Thomas Crowe was escalating his campaign against their operation, moving beyond territorial warnings to active dismantling of their intelligence network.

The timing couldn't be worse. After relocating to escape Veronica's hunters, they had spent weeks rebuilding their business infrastructure: finding new lodgings, establishing alternative routes to medical schools, and cultivating fresh informants. Just as they were regaining stability, Crowe had struck with precision at their most vulnerable point.

Without cemetery informants, they couldn't identify valuable burial sites or security weaknesses. Without that intelligence, their resurrection operations would become increasingly risky, less profitable, and potentially deadly.

Elizabeth left a coin on the table and departed

through the back entrance, taking a circuitous route back to their new lodgings, a small but secure set of rooms above a bookbinder's shop in a neighbourhood where residents minded their own business. The autumn air carried the familiar London mixture of coal smoke and Thames dampness, the evening fog already gathering in thick patches that offered welcome concealment.

Bob was waiting with tea already brewed, his expression shifting from relief to concern as he read her face.

"Bad news?"

Elizabeth removed her bonnet and gloves, settling into the worn armchair that represented one of their few comforts in these sparse quarters. "Crowe's men attacked Perkins, Wilson, and Whitby last night. Jenkins says they took Whitby's eye."

Bob's face hardened. "Sending a message."

"A very effective one," Elizabeth agreed grimly. "Jenkins won't work with us again, and I expect the others will distance themselves as well."

She accepted the cup Bob offered, the hot tea providing momentary comfort against the chill of their situation. Their new lodgings were more defensible than the previous rooms, with a solid door with multiple locks, windows that opened onto a narrow ledge rather than a public street, and alternative exits Bob had carefully identified. But physical security meant little if their business infrastructure collapsed around them.

"We could approach Crowe directly," Bob suggested. "Negotiate territorial boundaries, agree to his percentage demands."

Elizabeth shook her head. "This goes beyond simple business territory now. He's making an example of us, showing what happens to independents who don't immediately submit." She set down her cup with deliberate care. "Capitulation would only delay the inevitable. He'd demand more and more until we were effectively working for him."

"Then what? We can't operate without informants."

"No," Elizabeth agreed. "But neither can Crowe."

She crossed to the small desk that served as their planning centre, unfolding a map of London's cemetery districts. Coloured markings indicated territorial claims: red for Crowe's established areas, blue for their own operations, yellow for disputed territories, and green for unclaimed or minor gang regions.

"Crowe has attacked our information sources," Elizabeth said, her finger tracing specific locations. "We'll respond by targeting his most profitable operations."

Bob studied the map with growing comprehension. "The Guy's Hospital arrangement."

Elizabeth nodded. "Exactly. Crowe supplies Guy's with eight to ten specimens weekly—his most lucrative and consistent contract. The arrangement depends on specific delivery schedules and quality expectations." Her expression hardened with determination. "We're going to disrupt it systematically."

As darkness fell over London, they developed their counterstrategy by lamplight. Elizabeth's knowledge of medical school operations, gleaned from her father's business and enhanced through her own negotiations, provided insights into Crowe's arrangements that his own men might not fully appreciate. Bob's practical understanding of cemetery logistics identified vulnerabilities in Crowe's transportation methods.

Their plan took shape: approach Guy's Hospital with competing information, intercept Crowe's shipments when possible, and offer alternative supply arrangements at more favourable terms. The strategy would strain their limited resources but might sufficiently damage Crowe's primary income to force reconsideration of his aggressive campaign.

"This is business warfare," Bob observed as they finalised details. "Your father would approve."

Elizabeth's expression flickered at the comparison. "Perhaps. Though I doubt he ever faced quite this level of opposition."

"He had advantages we don't," Bob pointed out. "Established reputation, greater resources, connections throughout London."

"And we have advantages he lacked," Elizabeth countered. "We're smaller, more adaptable, and significantly less visible to authorities." She rolled up the map with decisive finality. "Besides, Crowe expects physical retaliation; violence answered with violence. He won't anticipate a strategic business response."

Later that night, as Bob slept on the narrow bed they still maintained separately despite their deepening relationship, Elizabeth remained awake, reviewing their resources and options. The conflict with Crowe had evolved from a territorial dispute to an existential threat, requiring a response that matched the gravity of their situation.

What troubled her most was not the business challenge but the human cost already accumulating.

Whitby had lost an eye for simply selling information about burial schedules. Others had suffered broken bones and worse. These weren't hardened criminals but working men trying to supplement meagre wages through relatively harmless intelligence selling.

Elizabeth had never intended to create collateral damage through her resurrection business. Yet people were being hurt; not by her directly, but because of her choices and her refusal to submit to Crowe's demands.

The moral calculation was becoming increasingly complex. Was defending their independent operation worth the suffering it caused to others? Yet surrendering to Crowe's territorial claims might only change which innocent people suffered, not whether they suffered at all.

With fog pressed against their windows, Elizabeth made her decision. They would proceed with their counterstrategy against Crowe's arrangement with Guy's Hospital, but with additional precautions to protect their remaining informants and associates. This was no longer merely about business survival but about establishing boundaries that even London's criminal hierarchy would respect.

* * *

"DR. WINTERS, might I have a moment of your time?"

The assistant anatomist at Guy's Hospital looked up from his paperwork, clearly annoyed at the interruption until he registered Elizabeth's refined appearance and speech. Her modest but well-maintained dress and articulate manner immediately distinguished her from the usual resurrectionists, all men, mind you, who approached the hospital's back entrances with their grim cargo.

"I'm rather busy, Miss...?"

"Smith. Elizabeth Smith." She offered the alias with practised ease. "I represent an alternative supply arrangement that might interest the hospital, particularly given recent inconsistencies in your current provisions."

Dr. Winters' eyebrows rose slightly. "I'm not aware of any inconsistencies."

"Three specimens last week showed advanced decomposition inconsistent with the documentation provided," Elizabeth stated confidently, though she had no specific knowledge of Crowe's recent deliveries. "And Tuesday's scheduled arrival was delayed by nearly six hours, disrupting your morning demonstration."

The anatomist's expression confirmed her calculated guess. Crowe's operation was indeed experiencing difficulties, likely due to increased police patrols Elizabeth had anonymously suggested to authorities for entirely different cemetery districts.

"These matters are handled by Dr. Phillips," Winters said, though his tone had shifted from dismissal to interest.

"Of course." Elizabeth produced a small card with an address where messages could be left. "When Dr. Phillips wishes to discuss more reliable arrangements at comparable rates, we would be pleased to demonstrate our capabilities."

She departed with unhurried dignity, knowing the seed had been planted. Similar approaches to other medical schools that maintained relationships with Crowe's operation would create doubt about his reliability precisely when his actual deliveries were being disrupted by Elizabeth and Bob's strategic interference.

The campaign continued over the following weeks. Bob's careful surveillance identified Crowe's transportation routes, allowing them to anonymously alert authorities to suspicious activities at precisely timed moments. Elizabeth cultivated relationships with cemetery workers outside Crowe's immediate influence, offering better compensation for exclusive information that allowed them to intercept potentially valuable specimens before Crowe's men could claim them.

Each small victory cost them precious resources: money for bribes and informant payments, time spent on surveillance rather than their own operations, and energy diverted from rebuilding their business to undermining Crowe's. But Elizabeth maintained their course with single-minded determination, recognising that half-measures would only prolong an unwinnable conflict.

The first sign of success came when Dr. Phillips contacted them himself through the address Elizabeth had provided. Guy's Hospital was experiencing concerning irregularities with its current supplier and wished to discuss alternative arrangements. The meeting was scheduled, terms negotiated, and a trial delivery arranged, all representing significant incursions into Crowe's most profitable territory.

"He'll retaliate," Bob warned as they prepared the specimens for their first Guy's Hospital delivery. "This strikes at his primary income."

"I'm counting on it," Elizabeth replied. "But he'll

need to identify the source of his troubles first. We've been careful to leave no direct evidence of our involvement."

Bob's expression remained troubled. "Crowe didn't become London's dominant resurrection man by being slow-witted. He'll connect the disruptions to us eventually."

Elizabeth knew he was right. Their campaign had been carefully orchestrated to obscure direct responsibility, but Crowe's network of informants and associates throughout London's criminal world made eventual discovery inevitable. The question wasn't whether he would identify them as the source of his troubles, but how he would respond when he did.

The answer came with shocking brutality three days later.

* * *

ELIZABETH WAS RETURNING from a successful negotiation with another of Crowe's former informants when she noticed the crowd gathered near the entrance to St. Catherine's Cemetery. The murmuring cluster of onlookers suggested something beyond ordinary interest, an accident, perhaps, or public disturbance.

She approached cautiously, maintaining the demeanour of a respectable young woman merely curious about the commotion. The crowd parted slightly, allowing her a glimpse of what had drawn their attention.

Murphy, the cemetery groundskeeper who had warned her about Veronica's hunters, lay crumpled on the cobblestones outside the cemetery gates. Blood pooled beneath his head; his face was so severely beaten that Elizabeth barely recognised him. Two constables stood nearby, questioning witnesses while waiting for a police wagon.

"What happened?" Elizabeth asked a woman standing beside her, fighting to keep her voice steady.

"Terrible business," the woman replied, clearly relishing the drama despite her disapproving tone. "Three men set upon the groundskeeper in broad daylight. Beat him something awful while folks watched. Said it was a message for someone he'd been talking to."

"Did they say who?" Elizabeth's mouth had gone dry, though she already knew the answer.

"Something about 'the girl and her boy,'" the

woman confirmed, eyeing Elizabeth with renewed interest. "You know something about it, miss?"

Elizabeth shook her head quickly and backed away, heart pounding against her ribs. This was no random violence or typical criminal intimidation. Attacking Murphy in public, in daylight, with witnesses present, represented a significant escalation in Crowe's tactics. He wasn't merely protecting territory now but sending a message that would resonate throughout London's criminal underworld.

The message was unmistakable: This is what happens to anyone who opposes Thomas Crowe.

Elizabeth returned to their lodgings by a circuitous route, checking repeatedly for followers although her mind remained fixed on the image of Murphy's broken body. Bob was out on reconnaissance, leaving her alone with the implications of what she had witnessed.

Their counter-campaign against Crowe had succeeded in damaging his operations but had provoked a response far more vicious than anticipated. Murphy had suffered not for providing current information, they hadn't worked with him since relocating, but simply for his past association with them. The public nature of the beating ensured maximum visibility, warning anyone who might consider assisting Elizabeth and Bob of the consequences.

When Bob returned hours later, Elizabeth recounted what she had seen, her voice steady despite the churning emotions beneath.

"This changes our calculations," she concluded. "Crowe has moved beyond business competition to public brutality. We need to consider whether continuing this conflict is justifiable."

Bob studied her with concern. "You're suggesting we yield to his demands?"

"I'm suggesting we evaluate whether our independence is worth the cost to others." Elizabeth's voice caught slightly. "Murphy may lose an eye, possibly his livelihood. For what? So we can operate without paying Crowe's percentage?"

The moral question hung between them, neither having an immediate answer. Their resurrection business had begun as desperate survival, evolved into modest prosperity, and now threatened to become the catalyst for escalating violence against innocent people.

"We should visit Murphy," Bob said finally. "At least ensure he has proper care."

The decision felt right, though Elizabeth recognised it as a postponement rather than a resolution of their larger dilemma. They would visit the injured man, provide what assistance they could, and perhaps gain clarity about their path forward.

* * *

THE CHARITY HOSPITAL where Murphy had been taken occupied a grim building in one of London's poorer districts. Inside, the atmosphere of suffering was palpable, presenting overcrowded wards, overworked staff, and the pervasive smell of carbolic acid barely masking the underlying odours of illness and poverty.

They found Murphy in a corner bed, his face bandaged so thoroughly that only one eye remained visible. That eye widened with recognition and fear when he saw them approach, his uninjured hand clutching the thin blanket as if seeking protection.

"We're not here to cause trouble," Bob said quietly, positioning himself to block the view of curious patients in nearby beds. "Just wanted to see how you're faring."

"Shouldn't be here," Murphy whispered hoarsely. "They said they'd finish the job if I spoke to you again."

Elizabeth moved closer, her chest tight with guilt

and anger. "We're sorry, Murphy. This happened because of us."

"Happened because of Crowe," he corrected, wincing as the movement disturbed his injuries. "Man's a devil. Always has been."

"The doctor's prognosis?" Elizabeth asked gently.

"Says I'll live." Murphy's attempt at a smile revealed missing teeth. "Won't be pretty, but I'll live. Right eye's gone, though. Can't work as a gravedigger with one eye; need depth perception for digging straight."

The matter-of-fact assessment of his diminished prospects struck Elizabeth more powerfully than any accusation could have. Murphy didn't blame them directly, yet his life had been irrevocably damaged by their conflict with Crowe.

"We'll help," she said impulsively. "With hospital costs, and after."

Murphy's visible eye studied her sceptically. "Kind offer, miss, but association with you is what got me here. Best we part ways clean."

The practical wisdom of his response didn't diminish its sting. Elizabeth placed several sovereigns on the small table beside his bed, more money than a cemetery groundskeeper might see in months.

"For your recovery. No expectations attached."

As they departed the hospital, Elizabeth's thoughts churned with conflicting emotions. Their visit had been motivated by genuine concern, yet it had also endangered Murphy further simply by association. The money might ease his immediate difficulties, but couldn't restore his eye or his livelihood.

"We're fighting a war we can't win," she said as they walked through streets growing dark with early autumn evening. "Crowe has more men, more resources, and more willingness to employ brutal violence."

"We've damaged his operation significantly," Bob pointed out. "The Guy's Hospital contract alone—"

"Is it worth it?" Elizabeth interrupted, stopping to face him directly. "Is our independence worth what happened to Murphy? Or Whitby? Or the others who've been hurt because they worked with us?"

Bob had no immediate answer, his expression reflecting the same moral uncertainty Elizabeth felt. They had begun their resurrection business out of desperate necessity, justified its continuation through rationalisation about medical progress, and now faced the human cost of their choices in ways that couldn't be easily dismissed.

"What are our alternatives?" he asked finally. "Submit to Crowe completely? Abandon London? Return to the streets with nothing?"

Elizabeth shook her head. "I don't know. But we need to consider whether we're becoming what we've fought against: people who accept others' suffering as collateral damage in pursuit of our own interests."

The parallel to her father's business methods, his casual disregard for the human consequences of his criminal enterprise, remained unspoken but present in her thoughts. William Flanders had justified grave robbing as serving medical science while treating his diggers as expendable resources. Was Elizabeth now following the same path, rationalising harm to others as necessary for her own survival?

They walked in troubled silence back to their lodgings, the moral question unresolved between them. But a new complication awaited; their land-lord, usually respectful of their privacy, intercepted them at the entrance with obvious discomfort.

"There's been talk," he said, glancing nervously up and down the street. "About your activities."

"What sort of talk?" Bob asked carefully.

"That you're not what you seem." The man lowered his voice further. "That the young lady reports to the police about other... businesses in the area."

Elizabeth's breath caught. This was a new and dangerous development since accusations of police informing represented a death sentence in London's criminal underworld.

"That's absolutely false," she stated firmly. "We operate our own modest enterprise and mind our business."

The landlord seemed unconvinced. "Maybe so. But the rumours are spreading. Three men came asking questions today. Rough sorts. I said nothing, but others might not be so discreet."

After assuring the landlord of their legitimate business status and providing additional rent in advance to secure his continued discretion, they retreated to their rooms. The implications of this new development were immediately clear to both of them.

"Crowe's spreading rumours," Bob said as he checked their security measures. "Turning the community against us."

Elizabeth nodded grimly. "A clever strategy. If other criminals believe we're informants, we become isolated, no one will work with us, sell to us, or protect us. We'd be vulnerable from all sides, not just Crowe's men."

The psychological warfare represented a more sophisticated attack than the physical beatings of their informants. By questioning Elizabeth's trustworthiness based on her refined background and manner, Crowe was weaponising the very class differences that had initially given her an advantage in their resurrection business.

Over the following days, evidence of the rumour campaign's effectiveness mounted. Contacts who had previously been reliable suddenly became unavailable. Shopkeepers who had extended small courtesies now regarded them with suspicion. Even cemetery workers with no direct connection to Crowe treated Elizabeth with visible distrust when she attempted to purchase information.

Simultaneously, Crowe's men intensified their physical presence near locations Elizabeth and Bob frequented, not directly threatening but maintaining visible surveillance that reinforced their vulnerability.

"He's dismantling everything we've built," Elizabeth observed as they assessed their dwindling options. "Not through direct confrontation but by isolating us from the community we depend on."

Their counter-campaign against Crowe's Guy's Hospital arrangement had succeeded in damaging his income but had provoked a response they were ill-equipped to combat. Without community connections, informants, or allies, their resurrection business would collapse regardless of how cleverly they operated or how determined they remained.

Elizabeth spread their map across the table, studying territorial markings that now seemed more aspirational than actual. Their blue areas had contracted significantly as Crowe's red expanded, pushing them toward the margins of viable resurrection territory.

"We need to reconsider our approach entirely," she said finally. "Conventional methods aren't working against Crowe's resources."

"What are you suggesting?" Bob asked, recognising the shift in her tone.

Elizabeth traced the boundaries of Crowe's territory thoughtfully. "He's expecting us to either escalate to his level of violence or withdraw completely. We need a third option; something unexpected that changes the fundamental dynamics of this conflict."

With the autumn rain drumming against their windows, Elizabeth began outlining a strategy so audacious that Bob initially thought she was joking.

But as she elaborated, connecting elements of her father's business methods with their own hard-earned knowledge of London's resurrection trade, the plan's dangerous brilliance became apparent.

"It's incredibly risky," Bob warned. "If it fails—"

"If it fails, we're no worse off than continuing this unwinnable conventional conflict," Elizabeth countered. "Crowe is systematically dismantling everything we've built. Without drastic action, we'll lose not just our business but potentially our lives when his rumours about police informing take full effect."

The plan would require careful preparation, perfect timing, and resources they could barely afford. It might destroy Crowe's operation entirely or provide him with the perfect opportunity to eliminate them permanently. There was no middle ground, no safe compromise position.

As they refined details late into the night, Elizabeth acknowledged to herself what she had been reluctant to admit earlier, that she had been fighting Crowe's war on his terms, allowing him to define the conflict through territorial thinking and escalating violence. Her education in her father's business methods should have taught her that true success came not from matching an opponent's strategy but from changing the nature of the competition itself.

Crowe operated through fear, violence, and traditional criminal hierarchies. Elizabeth would need to employ intelligence, strategic thinking, and unconventional approaches that her opponent couldn't anticipate or easily counter.

The rain continued its steady percussion against their windows as Elizabeth and Bob finalised their desperate gambit. Whether it represented brilliant strategy or suicidal recklessness remained to be seen, but one thing was certain: they had reached the point where conventional methods offered no path forward.

Tomorrow, they would begin implementing a plan that would either secure their position in London's resurrection trade or end their operation permanently. Elizabeth felt the weight of this decision, but also a strange clarity that had been missing during their reactive struggle against Crowe's systematic campaign.

They were no longer merely defending territory but fighting for their right to exist independently in London's criminal ecosystem. And while Elizabeth harboured no illusions about the morality of their resurrection business, she recognised that surrendering to Crowe's brutality would only ensure that violence continued under different management.

As she finally sought sleep in the early morning hours, Elizabeth's thoughts returned to Murphy lying in that charity hospital, his life irrevocably changed by their conflict. Whatever path they chose moving forward, she silently promised that his suffering would not be meaningless. It would become the catalyst for ending Crowe's reign of terror, one way or another.

CHAPTER 12

"The timing must be precise," Elizabeth said, reviewing their plan one final time as the thick winter fog pressed against the windows of their lodgings. "Crowe's men will be at Highgate Cemetery by midnight. The anonymous tip to Inspector Harrison must reach him by eleven, giving the police sufficient time to position themselves but not enough to be visible before Crowe's operation begins."

Bob nodded, checking the sealed note that would soon be delivered to the Metropolitan Police by a street urchin who knew nothing of its contents. "The message identifies only Crowe's men, locations, and methods. Nothing that could implicate our own operations."

Elizabeth studied their carefully drawn map of Highgate Cemetery, marking the Edwards burial plot where Crowe's team would be working tonight. After weeks of systematic attacks on their resurrection business, this counterstrike represented their most audacious gambit, using the authorities to eliminate their primary competitor while protecting their own activities.

"If this succeeds," she said, "Crowe's arrest will create temporary chaos in the resurrection trade. The medical schools will need alternative suppliers immediately."

"And we'll be positioned to fill that need," Bob finished. "With Crowe's reputation destroyed, we could reclaim our territories and expand beyond them."

The plan balanced on a knife's edge of risk and opportunity. Using the police as unwitting allies against Crowe might work brilliantly or fail catastrophically. Elizabeth had calculated every variable, anticipated every contingency. Yet unease lingered beneath her strategic confidence, a whisper of warning she couldn't quite silence.

"Something still troubles you," Bob observed, reading her expression with the familiarity born of months working side by side.

"It feels too simple," Elizabeth admitted. "Crowe has consistently outmanoeuvred us recently. His intelligence network is extensive. What if—"

A sharp knock interrupted her speculation. They exchanged glances, immediately alert. No one should be visiting at this hour, and their few remaining associates knew better than to approach directly.

Bob moved to the door, positioning himself defensively while Elizabeth retreated to the corner where their emergency funds and weapons were concealed. The precautions had become second nature during their conflict with Crowe.

"Message for Miss Smith," called a young voice from the hallway.

Their established alias. Bob opened the door cautiously to reveal a ragged boy of perhaps ten, clutching a folded paper.

"From Jenkins at St. Mary's," the boy announced. "Said it's urgent."

Elizabeth accepted the note with a small coin as payment. The boy disappeared down the stairs as she unfolded the paper, recognising Jenkins' rough handwriting despite his previous insistence that he would no longer communicate with them.

Her expression changed as she read, blood draining from her face.

"What is it?" Bob asked, alarmed by her reaction.

"Mrs. Eleanor Ashford has been murdered," Elizabeth said, her voice unnaturally calm despite the horror of the news. "And her body stolen from the grave."

Bob's brow furrowed. "Ashford... wasn't that—"

"Veronica's most recent victim," Elizabeth confirmed. "The wealthy widow she poisoned three weeks ago. The body was discovered missing this morning when relatives came to place flowers."

She handed him the note, mind racing with implications. Eleanor Ashford had been Veronica's latest target, an elderly widow whose suspicious death had followed the familiar pattern of gradual poisoning. Elizabeth had been monitoring the case from a distance, gathering evidence of Veronica's methods without directly intervening.

Now the body had vanished from its grave, transforming a suspicious death into something far more sinister.

"This can't be a coincidence," Elizabeth said, pacing the small room. "Not tonight of all nights, when we're moving against Crowe."

Bob studied the note with growing concern.

"Jenkins says there's unusual police activity around the cemetery. They're searching for suspects."

"We need more information," Elizabeth decided. "Our plan for Crowe must wait. This development changes everything."

They abandoned their carefully prepared ambush of Crowe's Highgate operation, instead venturing into the fog-shrouded streets to investigate this unexpected complication. Elizabeth's instincts screamed warning, the timing too perfect, the connection to Veronica too direct to be random chance.

As they approached St. Mary's Cemetery, the unusual activity became immediately apparent. Police constables patrolled the gates while small groups of onlookers gathered despite the late hour and winter chill, drawn by the excitement of criminal activity in their neighbourhood.

Elizabeth approached a woman on the fringe of the crowd, adopting the manner of a concerned local. "What's happened? All these police..."

"Grave robbery, they're saying," the woman replied eagerly. "But not the usual sort. The Ashford widow who died last month, someone dug her up and took her body. Left a right mess, they did."

"How dreadful," Elizabeth murmured. "Any idea who might have done such a thing?"

"Police seem to have some notion," the woman lowered her voice conspiratorially. "They're looking for a young woman, well-spoken but associated with the resurrection trade. Working with a young man, they say. Been asking questions all day."

Elizabeth maintained her expression of casual interest while her stomach tightened with dread. The description matched her and Bob precisely. This was no coincidence; someone had deliberately connected them to the Ashford grave robbery.

"How interesting," she managed. "What evidence do they have?"

"Tools left behind, apparently. Very distinctive ones, according to my husband, who works as a groundskeeper. And witnesses who saw suspicious figures near the cemetery last night." The woman leaned closer. "They say the body's been found already, in some warehouse connected to these resurrection people."

Elizabeth thanked the woman and moved away, signalling Bob to follow at a discreet distance. When they reached a quiet side street, she relayed what she'd learned, her voice tight with controlled panic.

"We're being framed," she concluded. "Someone has deliberately connected us to this crime."

"Crowe," Bob said with certainty. "He's turning our plan against us."

Elizabeth shook her head. "Not just Crowe. This involves the Ashford woman, Veronica's victim. The timing is too perfect, the connection too specific. They're working together somehow."

The realisation struck with devastating clarity. Veronica had been hunting Elizabeth for months. Crowe had been systematically destroying their resurrection business. Separately, they represented serious threats; together, they formed an alliance that Elizabeth had never anticipated.

"We need to see the grave," she decided. "Understand exactly what evidence has been planted."

"Too risky," Bob objected. "If the police are specifically looking for us—"

"We must know what we're facing," Elizabeth insisted. "Jenkins can get us in through the groundskeeper's entrance. We'll be careful."

Reluctantly, Bob agreed. They approached St. Mary's Cemetery from the service entrance, where Jenkins waited nervously, jumping at every shadow.

"I shouldn't be doing this," he muttered as he led

them through the darkened grounds. "Police have been questioning everyone who works here. They've got descriptions of you both."

"We appreciate the risk," Elizabeth assured him, pressing additional coins into his palm. "We just need to see what happened."

The Ashford grave stood in the cemetery's eastern section, surrounded by disturbed earth and the unmistakable signs of hasty excavation. Police had cordoned the area with rope, but in the darkness, Elizabeth could approach close enough to examine the scene.

What she saw confirmed her worst fears. The grave had been opened using techniques she and Bob had developed, including the distinctive shovel marks that minimised noise, and a particular approach to removing the coffin lid that left specific splintering patterns. Most damning of all, a small, specialised tool lay half-buried near the grave's edge, one of their custom implements, marked with the notch Elizabeth used to identify their equipment.

"That's my prying tool," she whispered in horror. "The one that went missing during the attack on our previous lodgings."

Bob examined the scene with growing alarm.

"They've studied our methods. Replicated them perfectly."

"Not just studied, they've been planning this for months," Elizabeth realised. "Since before the attacks on our informants began. This is why Crowe's men ransacked our rooms; not just to intimidate us but to acquire our tools and understand our techniques."

The implications were staggering. While Elizabeth had been developing counterstrategies against Crowe's business operations, he had been meticulously preparing a trap that would destroy her completely. The grave robbery was staged to implicate her using her own distinctive methods, while the connection to Mrs. Ashford as Veronica's victim suggested a level of coordination between her enemies that Elizabeth had never imagined possible.

"We need to leave London," Bob said urgently. "Tonight. The evidence against us is overwhelming."

Elizabeth nodded, her mind still processing the elaborate nature of the frame. "But first, we need to find where they've planted the body. The woman mentioned a warehouse connected to us."

"Too dangerous," Bob insisted. "If the police have already discovered it—"

"Then we're already implicated," Elizabeth countered. "But if we understand the full extent of the frame, we might find weaknesses, inconsistencies we could exploit."

They departed the cemetery as silently as they had entered, thanking Jenkins with a warning to distance himself from them immediately. The fog had thickened, providing welcome concealment as they made their way toward the Thames docklands, where several abandoned warehouses had occasionally served as temporary storage for their operations.

The police presence became apparent two streets away by lanterns piercing the fog and constables establishing a perimeter around a familiar building where Elizabeth and Bob had briefly stored specimens during the early days of their business. They watched from the shadows as officers carried a stretcher from the warehouse, a sheet-covered form clearly visible despite the darkness.

"They've found her," Elizabeth whispered, her last hopes collapsing. "Planted in a location directly connected to us."

"We need to go," Bob urged, tugging at her arm. "Now, before—"

"You there! Stop!"

The shout came from behind them as a constable emerged from the fog, lantern raised to illuminate their faces. More police appeared, summoned by their colleague's call, surrounding them with practised efficiency.

"Elizabeth Smith and Robert Miller?" the lead officer demanded, though his tone suggested he already knew the answer.

Elizabeth maintained her composure despite the crushing realisation that escape was impossible. "There's been a misunderstanding," she began.

"Save it for the magistrate," the constable interrupted, producing handcuffs. "You're both under arrest for grave robbery and suspicion of murder."

The cold metal closing around her wrists made the nightmare real in a way that even the planted evidence hadn't. Elizabeth stood motionless as the charges were formally stated, each word driving home the magnitude of the trap that had closed around them.

Not just grave robbery, which might result in transportation like her father, but murder. The accusation struck like physical force. They were being charged not merely with stealing Mrs. Ashford's body but with killing her before the theft.

"This is madness," Bob protested as he, too, was restrained. "We had nothing to do with any murder."

"The magistrate will hear your denials," the

officer replied dispassionately. "Though the evidence speaks rather conclusively."

As they were led toward the waiting police wagon, Elizabeth's analytical mind continued working despite her shock. The frame was more elaborate than she had initially realised. Not just connecting them to grave robbery but implicating them in Veronica's poisoning of Mrs. Ashford. Somehow, the investigation had been manipulated to suggest that Elizabeth had graduated from stealing corpses to creating them.

The pieces aligned with devastating clarity. Veronica's victim provided the body. Crowe's knowledge of Elizabeth's methods allowed for perfect replication of her techniques. Together, they had constructed a frame so convincing that even Elizabeth might have believed it herself had she not known the truth.

The journey to the police station passed in a blur of fog-muffled streets and the creak of wagon wheels. Elizabeth's mind raced through possible defences, explanations, and alibis, each disintegrating under the weight of the evidence against them. Her distinctive tools at the grave site. Witnesses who would swear they saw someone matching her description. The body found in a warehouse connected to their operations.

At the station, they were separated immediately, Bob's protests fading as he was led to a different holding area. Elizabeth answered the booking officer's questions mechanically, providing her alias while knowing it would soon be revealed as false. Her true identity as Elizabeth Flanders, daughter of the transported grave robber William Flanders, would only strengthen the case against her; criminal inheritance made manifest.

The holding cell was cold stone and iron bars, occupied by three other women who regarded the newcomer with varying degrees of curiosity and hostility. Elizabeth retreated to the corner farthest from them, sinking onto the wooden bench as the magnitude of her situation finally penetrated her strategic calculations.

She had been outplayed completely. While she had been developing clever countermeasures against Crowe's business operations, he had been constructing a trap so perfect that escape seemed impossible. The evidence against her was overwhelming, the charges capital in nature. At seventeen, Elizabeth faced the gallows for a murder committed by her stepmother and framed by her business rival.

The irony might have been appreciable had it not been so devastating. Her father had taught her to analyse business challenges systematically, to anticipate competitors' moves, and to think several steps ahead. She had applied those lessons brilliantly in building their resurrection business from nothing. Yet in this final, crucial conflict, she had been so thoroughly outmanoeuvred that her own strengths had become weaknesses.

Morning brought the magistrate's hearing, a brief, perfunctory affair where evidence was presented, charges formally laid, and Elizabeth and Bob remanded to Newgate Prison to await trial. The prosecution's case appeared overwhelming: Elizabeth's distinctive tools found at the grave site, multiple witnesses claiming to have seen a young woman matching her description near the cemetery, and the body discovered in a warehouse linked to their resurrection activities.

Most damning of all was the medical examiner's testimony that Mrs. Ashford had been poisoned before burial, not through natural causes as originally believed, but systematically over weeks with a combination of toxins that suggested calculated murder rather than disease. The prosecution presented a compelling narrative: a young woman corrupted by criminal inheritance who had escalated from stealing corpses to creating them for profit.

Elizabeth's refined manner and education, which had served her so well in building their resurrection business, now worked against her. The jury of working-class men viewed her as something worse than a common criminal, a fallen gentlewoman who had used her advantages for evil rather than good.

Bob's attempt to provide an alibi was dismissed as the obvious lies of an accomplice, his own criminal background undermining any credibility he might have had. The magistrate ordered them both held for trial at the Old Bailey, with proceedings to begin within the fortnight, given the serious nature of the charges.

As Elizabeth was led from the courtroom, a familiar face in the gallery caught her attention. Veronica sat in the back row, dressed in modest mourning clothes that suggested appropriate respect for the legal proceedings. Their eyes met briefly, Elizabeth's wide with recognition, Veronica's cool with satisfaction.

In that moment, Elizabeth understood the true depth of the conspiracy against her. Veronica had not merely provided the victim for the frame; she had actively participated in its construction, perhaps even suggested the strategy to Crowe. The woman who had murdered Elizabeth's mother, attempted to murder Elizabeth herself, and poisoned countless wealthy widows for profit had now engineered her stepdaughter's conviction for one of her own crimes.

The perfect symmetry of the trap closed around Elizabeth like iron bands. Accused of a murder she didn't commit, implicated by evidence too perfect to refute, facing a justice system more interested in swift conviction than truth, she had no apparent path to escape or vindication.

While the prison wagon carried her toward Newgate, Elizabeth caught a final glimpse of Veronica leaving the courthouse, a small smile playing at the corners of her mouth. The stepmother who had hunted her for months had finally achieved her goal. Elizabeth would hang for Veronica's crime, eliminating the last witness who could expose her murderous activities.

The gates of Newgate Prison closed behind the wagon with a finality that echoed in Elizabeth's bones. She had entered the same hell that had held her father years earlier, but under charges far more serious than his. William Flanders had been transported for grave robbery; his daughter would hang for murder.

In the cold confines of Newgate's women's section, Elizabeth forced her mind to continue working despite despair's crushing weight. She had been outplayed by the combined forces of Crowe's criminal expertise and Veronica's murderous cunning, but the game wasn't completely finished. Two weeks remained before her trial; two weeks to find some flaw in the perfect frame, some evidence that might at least cast reasonable doubt on her guilt.

Bob's anguished face in the courtroom gallery had communicated both devotion and helplessness. He would do everything possible to help her, but his options were as limited as her own. The trap had been too perfectly constructed, the evidence too overwhelming, the narrative too compelling for simple denials to overcome.

As darkness fell over Newgate, Elizabeth stared at the stone ceiling of her cell, the magnitude of her situation settling into her bones. She had survived Veronica's murder attempt, built a business from nothing, navigated London's criminal underworld with remarkable success, only to be destroyed by the combined efforts of her two most dangerous enemies.

The resurrection woman who had risen from desperate circumstances now faced her own mortality with bitter clarity. Unless some miracle intervened, Elizabeth Flanders would hang for a murder committed by her stepmother, her brief life ending in the same criminal shadow where it had been forced to exist.

CHAPTER 13

The condemned cell in Newgate Prison was a nightmare of cold stone, inadequate food, and the constant presence of death. Elizabeth shared the women's section with two other prisoners awaiting execution: a prostitute convicted of murdering her client and an older woman who had killed her abusive husband after twenty years of brutality. The daily routine was broken only by visits from the prison chaplain, who attempted to secure Elizabeth's confession and repentance for crimes she didn't commit.

"The Lord knows your sins, child," he intoned during his morning visit, Bible clutched to his chest like a shield. "Confession brings peace to the soul before its final journey."

Elizabeth regarded him steadily from her hard, wooden bench. "I cannot confess to murder, sir. I am guilty of many things, but not the death of Mrs. Ashford."

The chaplain sighed, adding her continued denial to his mental ledger of her sins. "Pride is a terrible companion on the scaffold, Miss Smith. Or should I say, Miss Flanders?"

Her true identity had been discovered shortly after her imprisonment. The daughter of William Flanders, a transported grave robber, now following her father's criminal path to its logical conclusion; the narrative was too perfect for authorities to question, too satisfying to public sensibilities to examine closely.

"Pride has nothing to do with it," Elizabeth replied. "Truth does."

When the chaplain departed, promising to return that evening for another attempt at saving her soul, Elizabeth returned to the letter she had been writing, a carefully worded appeal to a solicitor Bob had identified as potentially sympathetic to their case. The man had represented resurrection men before, understanding the distinction between grave robbery and murder.

Her fellow condemned prisoners watched with

varying degrees of interest. Martha, the prostitute, had abandoned hope entirely, spending her days in tearful prayers or catatonic silence. Agnes, the older woman who had killed her husband, maintained a stoic dignity that Elizabeth found herself admiring.

"Another appeal, dearie?" Agnes asked, her weathered face creasing with sympathy. "Best prepare your soul instead. They've made up their minds about us."

"Perhaps," Elizabeth acknowledged, continuing to write. "But while life remains, so does possibility."

Agnes nodded approvingly. "You've spirit, I'll grant you that. Waste of a sharp mind, hanging you."

Elizabeth appreciated the simple recognition of her intelligence. Throughout her trial, her educated manner and analytical thinking had been presented as evidence of calculated evil rather than natural ability. A young woman who spoke well and thought clearly must be especially dangerous, the prosecution had implied, particularly one who followed her father's criminal path.

The letter complete, Elizabeth set it aside for Bob's next visit. He came every afternoon, having sold everything they owned to bribe guards for extended visiting privileges. These brief encounters had become the centre of Elizabeth's existence, moments of connection in the isolation of her condemned status.

When Bob arrived that afternoon, Elizabeth immediately recognised the toll their separation had taken. His face was gaunt with worry, his clothes increasingly shabby as he spent every penny on her defence. Yet his eyes still lit with that particular warmth reserved only for her.

"Any news?" she asked after they were seated in the visiting area, a guard standing close enough to hear every word.

Bob shook his head slightly. "Mr. Hargrove reviewed the trial documents but says the evidence is..." he hesitated, glancing at the guard.

"Overwhelming," Elizabeth finished for him. "You can speak plainly, Bob. I harbour no illusions about my situation."

"He says without new evidence, an appeal has no chance of success." Bob's voice dropped lower. "I've approached three other solicitors. None will take the case without substantial payment."

Elizabeth nodded, unsurprised. Legal professionals who might work for charity were already convinced of her guilt by the overwhelming evidence. Those willing to represent the obviously guilty demanded fees far beyond Bob's means.

"What about the journalist?" she asked, referring to a newspaperman who had expressed interest in the case.

"Only interested in sensationalist aspects," Bob replied with disgust. "Wanted me to confirm rumours about your father's grave robbing business, create a story about criminal inheritance. Nothing that would help your case."

Elizabeth passed him the letter she had written. "Try Mr. Blackwood next. He represented resurrection men in the Smithfield case last year. He might understand the distinction between our actual activities and murder."

Bob tucked the letter into his jacket, his fingers brushing hers for a brief, forbidden moment. The guard cleared his throat warningly, and they separated, the small contact sustaining Elizabeth more than the meagre prison food.

"I won't stop trying," Bob promised as their time ended. "Every solicitor, every journalist, every person with influence, I'll approach them all."

Elizabeth managed a smile for his benefit. "I know you will."

But as he was led away, the reality of their situation pressed down upon her once more. Bob was selling everything, approaching everyone, exhausting himself in desperate efforts to save her, but his criminal background and lack of money made him an ineffective champion against the weight of evidence and prejudice.

Back in her cell, Elizabeth faced the growing probability that her execution would proceed as scheduled. Fourteen days had already passed since her conviction. The date was set for three days hence. Unless some miracle intervened, she would hang for Veronica's crime.

That night, after her cellmates had fallen into uneasy sleep, Elizabeth began a different kind of writing, not an appeal for help but a detailed confession of her real crimes. This document, intended for Bob to keep as a record of the truth, revealed the full scope of her transformation from innocent child to hardened criminal.

She acknowledged her grave-robbing activities, her role in building an illegal enterprise, and her moral compromises, but distinguished between her survival-driven crimes and the calculated murders of which she was accused. Writing this confession forced her to confront the person she had become and the choices that led to this moment.

I do not claim innocence in all things, she wrote by the dim light filtering through the cell's high window. *I have violated graves, disturbed the dead, and sold human remains for profit. These acts, born of desperate circumstance rather than malice, I freely confess and for them accept society's judgment. But I have never taken a living soul, never created death where there was life. Mrs. Ashford died by poison administered over weeks; the particular method favoured by my stepmother, Veronica Flanders, who has murdered numerous wealthy widows for their inheritances.*

The confession continued for pages, detailing Elizabeth's life from her first awareness of her father's criminal activities through her flight from Veronica's murderous intentions to her partnership with Bob and their resurrection business. She named names, provided dates, and described locations, creating a document that might someday exonerate her memory, if not save her life.

Dawn found her still writing, fingers stained with ink, eyes burning with fatigue, but mind clear with purpose. This record might be her only legacy, the sole testament to the truth of her life and circumstances.

* * *

The second day before her scheduled execution brought an unexpected visitor. Dr. Pemberton from St. Bartholomew's Hospital, who had been one of Elizabeth's regular customers for corpses. The prison officials, apparently impressed by his professional standing, allowed a private interview in a small room normally reserved for legal consultations.

"Miss Flanders," he greeted her, studying her prison-pale face with clinical interest. "You look remarkably composed for your circumstances."

"Did you come to observe the condemned, Doctor?" Elizabeth asked, her tone neutral. "Or is there some professional purpose to your visit?"

Pemberton settled into the chair opposite her, arranging his coat with precise movements. "Professional curiosity, primarily. Your methods and organisation were quite impressive; far beyond the typical resurrection operations we encounter. I wished to understand them better."

The true nature of his visit became clear: not sympathy but academic interest in her criminal techniques. Elizabeth might have been offended had she not recognised the opportunity this presented. Dr. Pemberton knew details about body procurement that could only come from someone currently active in the trade.

"You speak of my methods in the past tense," she observed carefully. "Yet I imagine the demand for specimens continues unabated."

"Indeed." Pemberton nodded. "Though your former territories have been quite efficiently absorbed by Mr. Crowe's organisation. He's implemented many of your approaches: the selective targeting of valuable specimens, the careful documentation, and the discrete delivery methods. Quite a remarkable transition."

Elizabeth maintained her composed expression despite the surge of bitter understanding. Crowe hadn't merely eliminated her as competition; he had studied her business model thoroughly, adopting her innovations to expand his own operation.

"And the quality?" she asked, professional pride momentarily overriding her circumstances.

"Comparable," Pemberton admitted. "Though the prices have increased substantially without competition. Mr. Crowe now enjoys a virtual monopoly on premium specimens."

Their conversation continued in this vein, a strange, detached discussion of the resurrection trade's current state that might have been a business meeting had it not occurred in a prison interview room. Elizabeth asked careful questions, gathering information about Crowe's operations and the medical schools' arrangements.

As their time ended, Pemberton regarded her with something approaching respect. "A waste of talent, your current situation. The medical profession has lost a remarkably efficient supplier."

"And an innocent woman may lose her life," Elizabeth replied pointedly.

Pemberton's expression flickered with momentary discomfort. "The evidence presented at trial seemed quite conclusive."

"Evidence can be manufactured, Doctor, as surely as medical knowledge can be advanced through the study of the dead." Elizabeth met his gaze directly. "Consider that some specimens appear natural in their death yet bear the marks of deliberate ending, if one knows where to look."

The doctor stood, gathering his hat and gloves. "An interesting observation, Miss Flanders. Though I fear beyond my professional purview at this juncture."

He departed with a formal nod, leaving Elizabeth to be escorted back to her cell. The information gleaned from their conversation confirmed her understanding of the conspiracy against her. Crowe had not merely framed her for murder but had systematically studied her business methods, positioning himself to absorb her innovation and clientele after her elimination.

The perfect crime: removing a competitor while simultaneously acquiring her business model and customers. Had the stakes not been her life, Elizabeth might have admired the strategic thoroughness of it.

That evening, Bob arrived for what might be their final visit before her execution. He had aged years in the weeks of her imprisonment, his young face lined with exhaustion and worry.

"Mr. Blackwood refused the case," he reported, the words clearly painful to deliver. "Says the evidence is too substantial to overcome without new information that would completely change the narrative."

Elizabeth had expected this response, but seeing Bob's despair made the news harder to bear. "You've done everything possible," she assured him. "More than anyone could expect."

"It's not enough." His voice cracked slightly. "I've failed you."

"No." Elizabeth leaned forward, ignoring the

guard's warning glance. "You've been my only ally, my only comfort. Whatever happens tomorrow, know that you gave me something precious: the knowledge that I wasn't alone."

Bob's eyes glistened with unshed tears. "I sold everything," he said quietly. "The tools, the records, our lodgings, everything to pay solicitors and bribes. But it wasn't enough to overcome..." He gestured helplessly, encompassing the weight of evidence and prejudice against them.

"I know." Elizabeth wished desperately that she could touch him, offer some physical comfort beyond words. "I've written something for you. A complete account of everything: our business, my father's activities, Veronica's murders. The truth, as best I can record it."

She had entrusted the document to a prison matron who had shown her small kindnesses, paying for its delivery to Bob with her last possession of value, a small silver ring that had belonged to her mother.

"I'll ensure it's not forgotten," Bob promised. "That someday, people will know the truth about what happened."

When their time ended, the parting held the weight of finality. Tomorrow's dawn would bring

Elizabeth's execution unless some miraculous intervention occurred. They both recognised the unlikelihood of such a reprieve.

"Live, Bob," Elizabeth said as the guard moved to escort her back to her cell. "Whatever happens to me, find a way to survive. That's all I ask."

He nodded, unable to speak, watching as she was led away, her back straight, her dignity intact despite the prison dress and chains. In that moment, Bob saw not the condemned prisoner but the remarkable young woman who had built a business from nothing, who had faced London's darkest elements with intelligence and courage, who had transformed his life through their unlikely partnership.

* * *

ELIZABETH'S final night in Newgate brought a visit from the prison chaplain, making a last attempt to secure her soul through confession. The man's persistence, while professionally motivated, contained genuine concern that a young woman might face eternity without proper spiritual preparation.

"The hour grows late, Miss Flanders," he said,

settling onto the small stool in her cell. "Tomorrow at dawn—"

"I'm aware of tomorrow's schedule," Elizabeth interrupted gently. "The gallows construction has been quite audible throughout the day."

The chaplain flushed slightly at her direct reference to the preparations for her death. "I come once more to offer spiritual comfort through confession. A clean soul meets its Maker with greater peace."

Elizabeth studied him thoughtfully. Throughout her imprisonment, she had maintained her innocence of murder while acknowledging her grave-robbing activities. The chaplain had heard this partial truth repeatedly but dismissed it as insufficient contrition. Tonight, with nothing left to lose, Elizabeth made a different decision.

"Would you hear the complete truth, Chaplain? Not just about my crimes but about those who framed me for murder?"

Something in her tone, a quiet intensity beyond her previous denials, caught the man's attention. "I would hear whatever you wish to share, child."

In the dim light of the cell's single candle, Elizabeth told him everything about Veronica's poisoning of her mother and subsequent murder attempts, her own flight and partnership with Bob, their resurrection business, and finally, the elaborate frame constructed through Veronica and Crowe's collaboration.

She spoke for nearly an hour, her narrative detailed and precise. The chaplain listened without interruption, his expression shifting from professional patience to growing disturbance as the account progressed.

"This is a most extraordinary tale," he said when she finished. "Yet told with such specificity..."

"Because it's true," Elizabeth replied simply. "I have committed many sins, Chaplain. I have robbed graves, disturbed the dead, and sold human remains. These crimes I freely acknowledge and for them accept judgment. But I did not murder Mrs. Ashford or anyone else."

The chaplain studied her face in the candlelight. "You understand that I cannot prevent tomorrow's sentence from being carried out."

"I understand. I don't seek intervention at this point, merely that the truth be recorded by someone who might eventually investigate my claims." Elizabeth met his gaze steadily. "Veronica Flanders continues to poison wealthy widows for their inheritances. Mrs. Ashford was merely one victim among many. Others will follow unless someone examines these deaths more carefully."

The chaplain was silent for several moments, weighing her words. "I cannot promise to investigate such claims myself, that lies beyond my duties. But I will record what you've told me, should evidence eventually emerge to support your account."

It was a small concession, unlikely to affect her fate, but Elizabeth accepted it gratefully. "Thank you."

After the chaplain departed, Elizabeth sat alone in her cell, listening to the muffled sounds of the prison at night, of other prisoners weeping or praying, guards making their rounds, and the occasional shout or cry from the men's section. Her cellmates slept fitfully, each dealing with their impending death in their own manner.

Elizabeth found herself strangely calm. The desperate hope for a last-minute reprieve had faded, replaced by a clear-eyed acceptance of what morning would bring. She had done what she could, recorded the truth for Bob, shared it with the chaplain, and maintained her dignity throughout. Whatever came next was beyond her control.

Her thoughts turned to her mother, wondering if Mary Flanders would recognise the woman her daughter had become. The innocent child who had first discovered her father's grave robbing business had transformed into someone who continued that same trade, albeit through different circumstances and choices. Yet Elizabeth believed her mother would understand the desperate decisions that led to this moment.

She thought too of her father, transported to Australia for the same crimes that formed the foundation of her own business. William Flanders had chosen his criminal path, and Elizabeth had been forced onto hers by circumstances. Yet the end result appeared remarkably similar, both judged and punished by a society that depended upon their services while condemning their methods.

The irony wasn't lost on her. The medical schools that purchased bodies from resurrectionists like her father, Bob, and herself were the same institutions that trained the doctors who would pronounce her dead tomorrow. The circular nature of death's business would complete itself through her execution.

* * *

DAWN ARRIVED with the sounds of the gallows being prepared in the prison yard. Elizabeth had slept little but felt strangely clear-headed as she rose and straightened her thin prison dress. The matron arrived with clean water for washing and a final meal that Elizabeth couldn't bring herself to touch.

"The chaplain will come shortly," the woman informed her, her tone professional but not unkind. "Then the procession to the yard."

Elizabeth nodded, appreciating the simple information without false comfort. "Thank you for your courtesies during my stay."

The matron paused, seemingly surprised by the polite acknowledgement. "You've been no trouble, miss. More dignity than most who pass through here."

It was a small recognition of the self-control Elizabeth had maintained throughout her imprisonment. She had not raged against her fate, attacked guards, or collapsed into hysteria like some condemned prisoners. Whatever her crimes, whatever injustice brought her to this moment, Elizabeth had refused to surrender the core of herself to Newgate's degradations.

When the chaplain arrived for final prayers, Elizabeth participated with quiet composure. The words meant little to her as religious comfort had never featured prominently in her life, but the ritual provided structure for these final moments.

"Is there anything you wish to say before we proceed?" the chaplain asked as he closed his prayer book. "Any final statement or request?"

Elizabeth considered the question carefully. "Only that the truth matters, even when justice fails. I hope someday that truth will be known."

The chaplain nodded solemnly. "I have recorded your account as promised. Whether vindication comes in this world or the next remains in God's hands."

The procession formed with methodical efficiency, guards, chaplain, Elizabeth, and more guards, moving through Newgate's cold corridors toward the yard where the gallows waited. Elizabeth walked steadily, refusing the chaplain's offered arm, her back straight and her gaze forward.

From the men's section came shouts and calls as word spread that a hanging procession passed. Elizabeth ignored these, focusing instead on placing one foot before the other, maintaining her composure for these final steps.

She thought of Bob, hoping he would find a way to survive and perhaps build the legitimate life they had sometimes discussed in quiet moments between operations. She thought of her mother, wondering if some reunion might await beyond death's threshold. She thought of Veronica, still free to continue her murderous activities, and Crowe, expanding his business using Elizabeth's innovations.

But mostly, Elizabeth thought about her own journey from privileged merchant's daughter to desperate fugitive to resurrection woman to condemned prisoner. Each transition had revealed aspects of herself she might never have discovered in a conventional life. Her intelligence, her adaptability, and her capacity for both moral compromise and ethical lines she would not cross.

As they approached the yard door, Elizabeth took a deep breath of the cold morning air that seeped through the cracks. She had made peace with her fate, understanding that her death was the logical conclusion of a life that began with her father's crimes and continued through her own moral compromises.

For now, she would face her execution with the dignity that had become her final possession. She would die for crimes she didn't commit, but she would do so as herself. Elizabeth Flanders, who had built something from nothing, who had loved and been loved by at least one person who saw her true worth, who had maintained her essential humanity despite the darkness that surrounded her.

The yard door opened, revealing the waiting gallows silhouetted against the grey January sky. Elizabeth stepped forward into the cold morning air, her final journey measured in yards rather than miles, her remaining time counted in minutes rather than years.

Whatever came next, oblivion or judgment or some unimagined continuation, she would meet it as she had faced life's challenges: with clear eyes, straight shoulders, and the quiet courage that had sustained her through London's darkest shadows.

CHAPTER 14

On the morning of Elizabeth Flanders' scheduled execution, a well-dressed stranger appeared at the law offices of Hartwell & Associates. His quality wool coat and polished boots distinguished him from the usual supplicants who waited hours for attention. The clerk hesitated only briefly when he gave his name as Mr. James Whitmore before informing a senior partner of his arrival.

"I apologise for appearing without appointment," Whitmore said when shown into the wood-panelled office of Mr. Charles Hartwell himself. His accent carried the distinctive cadence of Australia, refined but with colonial directness. "My business concerns a pending miscarriage of justice that cannot wait for proper scheduling."

Hartwell, a grey-haired man whose professional detachment masked a shrewd assessment of potential clients, noted the quality of the stranger's attire and the substantial purse he placed on the desk.

"A retainer," Whitmore explained, "to secure immediate representation in a matter of life and death."

The weight of the purse caught Hartwell's full attention. "What sort of justice concerns you, Mr. Whitmore?"

"The execution of an innocent woman, scheduled for this morning at Newgate." Whitmore's blue eyes held an intensity that belied his calm tone. "Elizabeth Flanders, convicted of murdering Mrs. Eleanor Ashford."

Hartwell's eyebrows rose slightly. "The Resurrection Girl case? The evidence was quite conclusive."

"Manufactured evidence," Whitmore corrected. "I have a witness who will testify that Miss Flanders was deliberately framed."

Before Hartwell could express his scepticism, the office door opened to admit Thomas Crowe, flanked by two rough-looking men whose purpose was clearly not social. Crowe's usual swagger had vanished, replaced by the wary tension of a trapped animal.

"Mr. Crowe has agreed to provide a full confession regarding his role in framing Miss Flanders," Whitmore said calmly. "Haven't you, Thomas?"

Crowe's eyes darted between Whitmore and the two men who stood close behind him. "I've been persuaded to correct certain misunderstandings," he muttered.

Hartwell stared at the tableau before him, professional curiosity overcoming his initial alarm. "This is most irregular, Mr. Whitmore."

"As is the execution of an innocent woman," Whitmore replied. "Time is short. Will you hear the testimony and act accordingly, or shall I seek assistance elsewhere?"

The substantial retainer and the extraordinary circumstances combined to overcome the lawyer's hesitation. "Proceed, Mr. Crowe."

Under the watchful eyes of his handlers, Crowe provided a detailed account of his conspiracy with Veronica Flanders. He described planting Elizabeth's distinctive tools at the grave site, arranging for false witnesses, and ensuring the stolen body was discovered in a warehouse connected to her operations.

"The Ashford woman was already dead," Crowe

explained, sweat beading on his forehead despite the winter chill. "Poisoned by someone else. We just took advantage to eliminate competition in the resurrection trade."

"And who suggested this particular method?" Whitmore prompted when Crowe fell silent.

"Veronica Flanders," Crowe admitted reluctantly. "The girl's stepmother. She provided information about the Ashford burial, suggested using it to frame Elizabeth. Said she had personal reasons for wanting the girl eliminated."

As Crowe's testimony continued, Hartwell summoned his associates. The gravity of the situation demanded immediate action regardless of how irregularly the information had been obtained.

"We must petition the Home Secretary immediately," Hartwell declared when Crowe had finished. "And present this evidence to the magistrates."

"There's no time for bureaucratic channels," Whitmore insisted, checking his pocket watch. "The execution is scheduled for nine o'clock. We must go directly to the Old Bailey with Crowe and his confession."

Hartwell hesitated only briefly before nodding to his associates. "Prepare the necessary documents. We leave immediately."

While the lawyers gathered their materials, Hartwell studied the mysterious Australian with new interest. "You've gone to extraordinary lengths to save a young woman with whom you claim no connection, Mr. Whitmore. May I ask why?"

Whitmore's expression revealed nothing beyond appropriate concern for justice. "Let us secure Miss Flanders' release first. Personal matters can wait until her safety is assured."

* * *

THE ROUGH HEMP of the noose scraped against Elizabeth's neck as the executioner adjusted it. She had been given a clean dress, a small dignity afforded the condemned, and her hair had been cut short to ensure the noose would sit properly. The cold morning air bit through the thin fabric, but she barely noticed, her senses oddly heightened yet distant.

The prison chaplain stood nearby, his prayers a meaningless murmur beneath the pounding of her heart. Elizabeth fixed her gaze on a patch of winter sky visible above the prison walls. Grey, like the stone of Newgate, like the faces of those who had come to witness her final moments.

A commotion erupted at the edge of the assembly. Raised voices, the rustle of papers. Elizabeth remained still, uncertain if this interruption was real or merely her mind creating a final desperate hope. The executioner paused, hands still on the noose.

The prison governor pushed through the crowd, accompanied by several men in legal attire. His face bore the pinched expression of a man whose carefully ordered schedule had been disrupted.

"The execution is stayed," he announced, voice tight with barely concealed irritation. "Remove the prisoner."

Elizabeth's legs nearly gave way beneath her. The noose scratched against her skin as it was lifted away, the sensation so vivid it brought tears to her eyes. Someone gripped her arm, the chaplain, his face a mixture of confusion and relief.

"What's happening?" Her voice sounded foreign, as if it belonged to someone else.

"New evidence has been presented," one of the legal men explained tersely. "You're to be returned to holding until the court reviews it."

Two guards led her away from the scaffold, her body moving mechanically while her mind struggled to comprehend this sudden reprieve. She had prepared so thoroughly for death that continued life seemed almost an intrusion, unwelcome yet desperately precious.

They took her to a small room near the administrative offices rather than back to the condemned cell. The walls were panelled wood instead of stone, the single window larger than those in the prison proper. Elizabeth sat on a hard wooden chair with her hands folded in her lap to hide their trembling.

Hours passed. The winter light shifted across the floor. Occasionally, voices filtered through the door of officials arguing about procedure, the shuffling of papers, and the distinct tones of legal debate. Elizabeth remained motionless, afraid that any movement might shatter this fragile moment between death and reprieve.

When the door finally opened, a grey-haired man in expensive legal attire entered. "Miss Flanders," he said, "I am Charles Hartwell. I represent new interests in your case."

Elizabeth stared at him, recognising him vaguely from her trial, though he hadn't been involved in her defence. "What interests?"

"A client who has brought forward evidence of your innocence." Hartwell placed a document before her. "Thomas Crowe has provided a full confession, detailing how he framed you in conspiracy with your stepmother, Veronica Flanders."

The names penetrated Elizabeth's shock. "Crowe confessed? Voluntarily?"

Something flickered across Hartwell's professional features. "His confession has been properly sworn and witnessed. The court has accepted its validity and overturned your conviction. You are to be released immediately."

Elizabeth's mind, temporarily suspended by the morning's emotional whiplash, began functioning again. "Crowe would never confess willingly."

"I am not privy to the circumstances that prompted Mr. Crowe's sudden attack of conscience," Hartwell replied carefully. "My concern is solely with securing your legal release."

He presented documents requiring her signature, explaining the terms with detailed precision. Elizabeth signed where indicated, her hand steadier than she expected. The formal process complete, Hartwell informed her that she would be free once the prison completed its administrative requirements.

"Someone will be waiting for you outside," he added. "A Mr. Miller, and my client, who facilitated today's proceedings."

"Your client? Who hired you to intervene in my case?"

"Mr. James Whitmore," Hartwell replied. "An Australian gentleman. Beyond that, I suggest you direct your questions to him directly."

The name meant nothing to Elizabeth, yet Hartwell's careful phrasing suggested he knew more than he revealed. Before she could press further, he departed, leaving her alone with the disorienting reality of her unexpected freedom.

The prison's release procedures passed in a blur of paperwork and returned possessions. The dress she had worn at her arrest hung loosely on her frame after weeks of prison rations. Her skin felt papery beneath her fingers, her wrists thin and fragile.

When the final gate unlocked, Elizabeth stepped into the winter sunlight outside Newgate. The brightness hurt her eyes after the prison's perpetual gloom. The air carried the sharp scent of coal smoke, horse dung, and the faint sweetness of roasting chestnuts from a vendor's cart. Ordinary London smells that now seemed extraordinary.

Bob waited at the bottom of the steps, his face a study in disbelieving joy. When their gazes met, he moved toward her with urgency, as if afraid she might vanish.

"Elizabeth." Her name carried all the emotion he couldn't express in public. "You're really free."

"Apparently so," she replied, her voice steadier than she felt. "Though I don't fully understand how."

They stood facing each other, maintaining proper distance while their eyes communicated everything words couldn't convey. Bob looked thinner, his clothes more worn, his face gaunt with worry. But his eyes held the same unwavering devotion that had sustained her through her darkest moments.

"A man came to our old lodgings looking for me," Bob explained. "Said he could help you if I told him everything about Crowe and your stepmother. I thought it was a trap at first, but he knew details about your father, about Australia. Said he could make Crowe confess."

A tall figure approached from a waiting carriage, a well-dressed man of perhaps forty-five, his bearing confident without ostentation. Something about his features tugged at Elizabeth's memory, though she couldn't immediately place him.

"Miss Flanders," he said, his Australian accent

immediately apparent. "I'm pleased to see you safely released. James Whitmore, at your service."

He extended his hand, which Elizabeth accepted automatically while studying his face. There was something familiar in his blue eyes, in the set of his jaw; echoes of someone she had known long ago.

Her skin prickled with awareness, a sensation that had nothing to do with the cold air. This man had arranged her rescue, yet his identity and motives remained unclear.

"You arranged for Crowe's confession," she said. "Why would an Australian gentleman involve himself in my case?"

Whitmore glanced at their surroundings. The street outside Newgate was hardly suitable for private conversation. "Perhaps we might continue this discussion somewhere more comfortable? I've taken rooms at the Great Western Hotel where we could speak freely."

Elizabeth hesitated. This man had saved her from the gallows, yet caution was deeply ingrained after years of survival on London's streets. "Bob comes with me," she said firmly.

"Of course," Whitmore agreed, seeming unsurprised by her condition. "Mr. Miller has been invaluable in providing the information needed to secure your release."

The carriage ride passed in silence, Elizabeth too overwhelmed to engage in conversation. Every sensation seemed amplified: the leather seats cold beneath her thin dress, the clatter of hooves on cobblestones nearly deafening, the passing buildings a blur of brick and stone.

Bob sat beside her, his solid presence anchoring her amid the unreality of her situation. Occasionally, his hand brushed against hers, a brief touch that conveyed more comfort than words could have provided. Whitmore observed them both with an expression Elizabeth couldn't quite interpret; interest certainly, but tinged with something more complex.

At the hotel, they were shown to a private sitting room where a meal had been arranged. The sight of proper food, roast beef, potatoes, and fresh bread reminded Elizabeth how inadequate prison rations had been. Her stomach clenched painfully, torn between hunger and the knowledge that eating too quickly after near-starvation would make her ill.

Whitmore encouraged them to eat before beginning serious discussion, watching with what appeared to be satisfaction as Elizabeth forced herself to take small, measured bites despite her body's demands for more.

When they had finished and tea was served, Whitmore finally addressed the questions evident in Elizabeth's careful observation of him.

"You don't recognise me," he said. "I'm not surprised. Eight years is a long time, and Australia changes a man in ways beyond the physical."

Elizabeth's cup halted halfway to her lips, her mind racing through implications. Eight years. Australia. The familiar features suddenly aligned in her memory, overlaying this prosperous gentleman with the father who had been transported when she was nine years old.

"Father?" The word emerged as barely more than a whisper.

William Flanders, for it was indeed he beneath the identity of James Whitmore, inclined his head in acknowledgement. "Hello, Elizabeth."

The teacup rattled against the saucer as Elizabeth set it down. Her throat constricted, a flood of memories washing through her of her father being led away in chains, Veronica's cruel smile as she claimed the house and business, years of believing herself truly alone in the world.

"How?" she asked, her voice unsteady. "You were transported for fourteen years."

William smiled slightly. "Australia offers opportunities for men with certain skills and determination. My sentence was commuted for 'exemplary behaviour and service to the colony.' The authorities there are more pragmatic than their London counterparts."

"You arranged Crowe's confession," Elizabeth said, connecting pieces of this extraordinary development. "How?"

"Money opens many doors," William replied. "And when financial persuasion proves insufficient, other methods exist." His tone suggested experiences Elizabeth could only imagine. "When news reached me of your situation, that my daughter faced hanging for a murder she didn't commit, I made immediate arrangements to return to London."

"How did you even know?" Elizabeth pressed. "We've had no contact since your transportation."

"I maintained certain connections in London," William explained. "When the 'Resurrection Girl' case made headlines, associates recognised the Flanders name. I received detailed reports about your trial and conviction."

Elizabeth absorbed this information, her analytical mind working through implications despite her emotional turmoil. Her father had not only survived transportation but had thrived, establishing sufficient wealth and influence to return to London and orchestrate her rescue through means both legal and otherwise.

The man before her was both familiar and a stranger. His eyes were the same blue she remembered, but now they held a hardness that spoke of experiences she could not fathom. His hands, once calloused from work with corpses and tools, now bore the manicured appearance of a gentleman. Even his voice had changed, acquiring the distinctive rhythms of Australia layered over London's cadences.

"What happens now?" she asked, the practical question emerging from dozens she might have voiced.

William leaned forward, his expression serious. "That depends on what you want, Elizabeth. I've secured your freedom, but London remains dangerous for you. Veronica still lives in your former home, and while Crowe has been temporarily neutralised, his organisation continues. Both would prefer you permanently silenced."

"You're suggesting I leave London," Elizabeth concluded.

"I'm offering you passage to Australia," William confirmed. "And partnership in my enterprises there. Legitimate businesses, primarily import-export, property development, shipping. The colonies reward intelligence and determination, qualities you clearly possess."

The proposal hung in the air between them. Escape from London's dangers. A fresh start in a new country. Financial security through partnership with her father. Freedom from the constant fear of Veronica's hunters or Crowe's vengeance.

Yet she felt Bob tense beside her, though he remained silent. His presence reminded her of everything they had built together, of the partnership that had evolved from necessity to something far deeper.

"And if I choose to remain in London?" Elizabeth asked, watching her father carefully.

"Then I would provide sufficient funds to establish you securely," William replied without hesitation. "Though I would caution against it. Veronica is still dangerous and will eventually seek revenge for this humiliation."

Elizabeth glanced at Bob, whose expression

remained carefully neutral despite the tension evident in his posture. He would never ask her to choose him over safety, over the opportunity her father presented. His silence conveyed both his love and his unwillingness to influence a decision that must be hers alone.

"I need time to consider," she said finally. "Today has been... overwhelming."

William nodded, unsurprised by her response. "Of course. I've taken rooms for you both here, separately but adjacent, to maintain proprieties. Rest, recover your strength, and consider your options. My ship departs in one week, should you choose to accompany me."

As he rose to leave them to their considerations, Elizabeth was struck by how completely their positions had reversed from her childhood. Then, William had been the authority figure whose decisions shaped her life. Now, she was an adult making choices her father could only present, not dictate.

"Why did you really come back?" she asked as he reached the door. "After eight years of silence, why risk returning to London where your own criminal past might be discovered?"

William paused, something vulnerable briefly visible beneath his confident exterior. "Because you're my daughter," he said simply. "And whatever else I may be, whatever crimes I've committed, I could not allow Veronica's final victory to be your death."

After he departed, Elizabeth and Bob sat in silence, the enormity of the day's events settling around them. From condemned prisoner to free woman in the space of hours. From orphaned criminal to daughter with a father offering prosperity and safety. From resigned acceptance of death to a future suddenly wide with possibilities.

"You should go with him," Bob said finally, breaking the silence. "Australia offers a fresh start, away from Veronica and Crowe. You'd be safe there."

Elizabeth studied him, noting the conflict between his words and the emotion evident in his eyes. "And what about you? What about everything we've built together?"

"We built a resurrection business that nearly got you hanged," Bob replied with uncharacteristic bitterness. "Hardly worth preserving at the cost of your safety."

"It wasn't just a business," Elizabeth said quietly. "It was survival. Partnership. Trust when neither of us had reason to trust anyone."

Bob met her gaze, his resolve visibly wavering. "I

want what's best for you, Elizabeth. If that's Australia with your father—"

"I don't know what's best yet," she interrupted. "I need time to think clearly, to understand what this means." She reached across the table to take his hand, propriety forgotten in the intimacy of shared survival. "But I won't make any decision without considering us both. That I promise you."

Outside the hotel windows, London continued its winter existence, carriages rattling over cobblestones, vendors calling their wares, the eternal rhythm of the city that had nearly claimed Elizabeth's life yet had also shaped her into the woman she had become.

One week to decide between safety in a distant land with a father newly returned from the past, or uncertain freedom in familiar streets with the man who had stood beside her through London's darkest shadows.

CHAPTER 15

"I'm staying in London."

Elizabeth's words hung in the morning air of William's hotel sitting room. Outside, February sunlight struggled through London's perpetual coal haze, casting weak patterns across the carpet. She had spent a week considering her father's offer of passage to Australia and partnership in his colonial enterprises, a week of weighing safety against connection, prosperity against purpose.

William's expression revealed genuine surprise. He set down his teacup with deliberate care. "May I ask why? London holds considerable danger for you. Veronica remains at large, and while Crowe's confession has secured your freedom, his associates may seek retribution."

"Those dangers exist," Elizabeth acknowledged. "But this is where I'm needed."

She had arrived at her decision the previous night, after hours of conversation with Bob and solitary reflection. The clarity that came with it brought unexpected peace and a certainty she hadn't felt since before her arrest.

"Bob is here," she continued. "We've built something together that goes beyond business partnership. And there are others, children living on London's streets as we once did, with no options beyond crime or destitution."

William studied his daughter with new awareness. The frightened girl he had left behind eight years ago had become a young woman of remarkable resilience and moral complexity. Her experiences, grave robbing, imprisonment, and near execution might have broken a weaker spirit. Instead, they had forged something stronger.

"You understand the risks," he said. It wasn't a question.

"Better than most," Elizabeth replied. "I've seen London's darkest corners. But I've also found connection and purpose here that I'm unwilling to abandon."

William nodded slowly. "Then I respect your

decision, though it differs from my recommendation." He reached into his coat, withdrawing a folded document. "This is a bank draft for five thousand pounds, drawn on my London accounts. Regardless of whether you accompanied me to Australia, this money was always intended for you."

Elizabeth stared at the document, the sum representing wealth beyond anything she had imagined. "This is—"

"Blood money, in many ways," William interrupted with unexpected candour. "Earned through methods neither of us should romanticise. But it can provide security while you establish whatever future you envision."

She accepted the draft, the paper surprisingly light for the weight it represented. "Thank you."

"There's something else I must do before departing," William said, his tone shifting toward business. "Veronica cannot be allowed to continue her activities. I've gathered considerable evidence of her poisonings; not just your mother, but at least seven other victims I've documented."

Elizabeth's breath caught. "You've been investigating her?"

"Since learning of your situation. My associates have been quite thorough." William's expression hardened. "The authorities will receive a comprehensive dossier tomorrow, including witness statements, financial records showing suspicious inheritances, and medical opinions regarding the poisoning methods."

"Will it be enough?" Elizabeth asked, hope and scepticism warring within her.

"Combined with Mrs. Hartwell's testimony about her own near poisoning, yes. Veronica's careful façade will crumble under proper investigation." William's confidence left little room for doubt. "Justice for Mary and for you will be served before I depart."

As their conversation continued, Elizabeth found herself studying this transformed version of her father. The grave robber who had introduced her to death's business had become something more complex; still morally ambiguous, still operating outside conventional boundaries, but with a code and purpose she hadn't recognised in her childhood.

"What will you do with the money?" William asked as their meeting drew to a close.

Elizabeth had been considering this question throughout their conversation. "Establish a foundation for London's street children. A place that offers shelter, education, and legitimate employment opportunities."

William's eyebrows rose slightly. "Charitable work? I wouldn't have predicted that direction."

"Not mere charity," Elizabeth corrected. "Practical intervention in cycles of poverty and crime. Children become resurrection workers, pickpockets, or worse because legitimate options are closed to them. I intend to create alternatives."

Understanding dawned in William's eyes. "You're building the path you wish had existed for you and Bob."

"Precisely." Elizabeth met her father's gaze directly. "The Flanders name has been associated with criminal enterprise long enough. I intend to transform its meaning."

William's laugh held genuine appreciation. "You continue to surprise me, Elizabeth. I believe you'll succeed." He rose, extending his hand formally. "I sail in three days. Should you ever reconsider Australia, you'll be welcome."

Elizabeth took his hand, the gesture bridging the years of separation and the moral complexities that defined their relationship. "Thank you for my life," she said simply. "Both for your intervention with

Crowe and for the resources to build something meaningful from it."

After William departed, Elizabeth remained in the sitting room, the bank draft still in her hand. The sum represented both opportunity and responsibility; blood money indeed, as her father had acknowledged, but now hers to redirect toward redemptive purpose.

Bob found her there, hesitating in the doorway until she beckoned him inside. "You told him?"

Elizabeth nodded. "He accepted my decision more readily than expected."

"And provided generous means to implement it," Bob observed, glancing at the bank draft still in her hand. "Five thousand pounds would buy passage to Australia many times over."

"It will establish the foundation instead," Elizabeth said, her voice strengthening with conviction. "The Flanders Foundation for Street Children, offering what we never had."

Bob's expression softened as he took the seat William had vacated. "You've been planning this."

"Since the night before my scheduled execution," Elizabeth admitted. "When I thought death inevitable, I found myself wishing I'd had opportunity to help others avoid our path. Now, improbably, I have both life and means to fulfil that wish."

They spent the morning outlining their vision, practical details emerging from Elizabeth's organisational mind and Bob's street knowledge. By afternoon, their plan had taken an initial shape of a building in a strategic location, programs combining education with practical skills, and outreach to children most vulnerable to criminal recruitment.

Three days later, William Flanders departed for Australia, leaving behind both his daughter and a legal storm that would soon engulf Veronica. The evidence he provided to authorities proved devastating, a meticulous dossier documenting her systematic poisoning of wealthy widows, financial records showing suspicious inheritances, and medical testimony regarding the distinctive toxin combinations she employed.

Veronica's arrest and subsequent trial became a sensation that eclipsed even the "Resurrection Girl" case. Elizabeth attended one session, watching from the public gallery as her stepmother's perfect composure finally cracked under the weight of irrefutable evidence. Their eyes met briefly across the crowded courtroom. Veronica's filled with cold hatred, Elizabeth's with the quiet satisfaction of justice long delayed.

The verdict surprised no one: guilty on multiple counts of murder by poisoning. The sentence followed swiftly, execution by hanging, the same fate from which Elizabeth had narrowly escaped. When the news reached her, Elizabeth felt no triumph, only a solemn recognition that one chapter of her life had finally closed. Her mother and Veronica's other victims had received justice, though too late for their own salvation.

* * *

SPRING SUNLIGHT STREAMED THROUGH NEWLY INSTALLED windows, illuminating dust motes dancing above freshly sanded floors. The building that would house the Flanders Foundation had previously been a disused warehouse in a neighbourhood balanced precariously between respectability and destitution; precisely the location Elizabeth had sought for their work.

"The dormitories will be completed next week," she informed Bob as they walked through the renovations. "Twenty beds initially, with capacity to expand as funding allows."

Bob nodded, his practical knowledge of construction evident in his assessment of the work. "The classroom space is well situated for natural light. Most of these children will never have studied in proper conditions."

The transformation of the building mirrored Elizabeth's own evolution from abandoned structure to purposeful space, from neglected resource to centre of possibility. Workers moved efficiently through the rooms, installing partitions, repairing plaster, and creating order from previous chaos.

"Miss Flanders?"

Elizabeth turned to find the project foreman approaching, his expression troubled. "Is there a problem, Mr. Harrison?"

"Some local concerns about your intentions," the man explained awkwardly. "Word has spread that you're establishing a place for street children. Certain neighbours worry about... undesirable elements being attracted to the area."

Elizabeth had anticipated such resistance. "Please invite any concerned parties to meet with me directly. I'll explain how our work will benefit the entire neighbourhood by reducing vagrancy and petty crime."

As Harrison departed, Bob gave her an appreciative glance. "You've become quite the diplomat."

"Necessity," Elizabeth replied with a small smile. "Our work requires community support to succeed. Fear and misunderstanding must be addressed directly."

They continued their inspection, discussing practical details of the foundation's operation. Elizabeth had spent weeks researching similar institutions, identifying both successful approaches and pitfalls to avoid. Her experiences on London's streets provided insights no conventional charitable organiser could match.

"We'll need staff soon," Bob noted as they examined the kitchen facilities. "People who can work with children from difficult circumstances without judgment or naivety."

"I've begun interviews already," Elizabeth said. "Former street children who've established legitimate lives make ideal mentors. They understand both worlds."

Their planning continued through spring and into summer, the foundation taking shape through Elizabeth's organisational skills and Bob's practical knowledge. By July, the building stood transformed with dormitories with actual beds rather than straw pallets, classrooms equipped with proper materials, workshops where practical trades could be taught, and a dining hall offering regular meals to children who had known only irregular scraps.

The Flanders Foundation officially opened on a warm August morning. Elizabeth stood at the entrance, watching as the first group of street children arrived, wary, suspicious, drawn by rumours of food and shelter but expecting some hidden cost for such provision.

A small boy of perhaps nine hung back from the others, his thin face a mask of calculated indifference that failed to hide his desperate hope. Elizabeth approached him directly, crouching to meet his eyes.

"You don't have to stay if you don't wish to," she said quietly. "But there's breakfast inside, a bed that's yours alone, and people who'll teach you skills beyond picking pockets."

The boy's eyes widened slightly at her direct reference to theft. "How'd you know—"

"I lived on these streets once," Elizabeth told him simply. "I know what survival requires when legitimate options are closed."

Something in her tone, the authenticity of shared experience rather than condescending charity, reached the child. He gave a barely perceptible nod and followed her inside, where Bob was already organising the other children with the natural authority of someone who understood their experiences.

That first day established patterns that would define the foundation's work. Children arrived hungry, suspicious, and defensive. They tested boundaries, hoarded food, concealed possessions, and prepared for inevitable disappointment. Elizabeth and Bob responded not with punishment or sermon but with consistent boundaries, practical education, and the quiet understanding that came from having walked similar paths.

"Why are you doing this?" a girl asked Elizabeth bluntly during the second week. Thirteen years old but with eyes far older, she had arrived with bruises suggesting experiences Elizabeth could well imagine. "What's your angle?"

"No angle," Elizabeth replied, continuing to sort donated clothing. "Just creating the alternative I wish had existed when I was your age."

"You wasn't never like us," the girl challenged, eyeing Elizabeth's now-respectable appearance.

Elizabeth rolled up her sleeve, revealing a thin scar that ran from wrist to elbow. "Knife fight, Covent Garden market, 1852. Man tried to take what little I had." She met the girl's gaze directly. "I was exactly like you. The difference is what happened afterwards."

The girl studied her with new awareness. "What happened?"

"Someone helped me when they could have walked away," Elizabeth said simply. "Now I'm doing the same."

This pattern repeated as children gradually accepted that the foundation offered genuine opportunity rather than exploitation or temporary charity. Elizabeth's background gave her insights conventional philanthropists lacked, understanding which rules mattered and which could bend, recognising when theft stemmed from genuine need rather than defiance, and distinguishing between necessary street toughness and dangerous behaviour.

Bob proved equally effective, particularly with boys who responded to his practical approach and obvious street knowledge. He taught reading alongside self-defence, mathematics with lessons on avoiding exploitation, and trade skills that offered alternatives to criminal activity.

As autumn approached, the foundation had established itself as a presence in the neighbourhood. Thirty-seven children now lived in the dormitories, with dozens more receiving day services. Local businesses had begun offering apprenticeships to older children who demonstrated reliability, creating pathways to legitimate employment that would have been unimaginable months earlier.

One evening, after the younger children had been settled for the night, Elizabeth found Bob on the roof, gazing across London's chimney-dotted landscape as gas lamps created islands of yellow light in the gathering darkness.

"Thinking about your father?" he asked as she joined him.

"Oddly enough, yes," Elizabeth admitted. "I received a letter today. He's established himself successfully in Melbourne. Legitimate businesses, primarily, though I suspect some enterprises might not bear close examination."

Bob smiled slightly. "The Flanders approach to redemption, gradual rather than absolute."

"Perhaps that's the only realistic path," Elizabeth mused. "Complete transformation happens rarely, if ever. We simply redirect our natures toward better purposes."

They stood in companionable silence, the city stretching around them in all directions. Somewhere in that maze of streets, they had once scrabbled for survival through grave robbing and body selling. Now they stood above it, not removed from its realities but engaged with them in fundamentally different ways.

"I've been thinking," Bob said finally. "About us."

Elizabeth turned toward him, noting the unusual hesitation in his normally direct manner. "Yes?"

"We've been partners for years now. In business, in survival, in this foundation." He gestured toward the building beneath them. "But there's no formal recognition of what we are to each other."

"Are you proposing marriage, Bob Miller?" Elizabeth asked, a smile tugging at her lips despite her attempt at seriousness.

"Inelegantly, it seems," he admitted, his expression both vulnerable and determined. "But yes. I am."

Elizabeth took his hand, the gesture natural after years of partnership that had evolved far beyond their initial alliance of necessity. "I accept, inelegance and all."

Their marriage took place in the foundation's main hall rather than a church, witnessed by the children they worked with rather than conventional society. Elizabeth wore a simple blue dress rather than traditional white, and Bob a suit purchased specifically for the occasion. The ceremony itself was brief, the celebration afterwards joyous in its lack of pretension.

"Mrs. Miller," Bob said experimentally when they finally found a moment alone.

Elizabeth shook her head. "I'll remain Flanders professionally. The foundation carries the name, and there's symbolic importance in reclaiming it for constructive purpose."

"Elizabeth Flanders in public, Mrs. Miller in private," Bob suggested, his smile warming his eyes. "A fitting arrangement for a woman who has always navigated multiple worlds."

Their married life developed as naturally as their partnership had evolved, each day building upon the foundation of trust and shared purpose they had established through years of working side by side. Their quarters at the foundation provided modest comfort and privacy while keeping them connected to the work that defined their shared mission.

* * *

THREE YEARS LATER, Elizabeth stood beside her mother's grave on a clear spring morning. The headstone, once neglected, now stood properly maintained, with fresh flowers from the foundation's garden arranged in a simple vase. At twenty-two, Elizabeth had grown into a woman of quiet confidence, her features matured from the desperate girl who had fled Veronica's murderous rage five years earlier.

"I think you would approve, Mother," she said softly to the silent stone. "Not of everything; there are chapters in my life that would horrify you. But of what we've built now, of the children we've helped, of the cycles we've broken."

The Flanders Foundation had expanded beyond its initial scope, now operating three facilities across London and providing services to hundreds of children annually. Elizabeth's organisational skills and Bob's practical knowledge had created an institution respected even by conventional philanthropic societies, though its methods sometimes raised eyebrows among more traditional charities.

"Elizabeth." Bob's voice called softly from the cemetery path. "Sorry to interrupt, but there's a situation requiring your attention."

She turned to see him approaching, a folded paper in his hand. At twenty-five, Bob had developed a quiet authority that commanded respect without intimidation, a valuable quality in their work with children accustomed to both neglect and abuse.

"What's happened?" she asked, touching the headstone briefly in farewell before moving to meet him.

"Police found a group of children living in the abandoned brewery near Whitechapel," Bob explained, handing her the note. "Six of them, ages seven to thirteen, apparently operating a small pickpocketing ring. The inspector remembered our work with similar cases last year."

Elizabeth scanned the message, her mind already calculating logistics, bed availability, staff requirements, and particular needs these children might present. "We'll need to assess them individually. The older ones may have established hierarchies we'll need to understand."

Bob nodded, familiar with their protocol for integrating new children. "I've already asked Sarah to prepare the intake rooms. The carriage is waiting."

As they walked through the cemetery toward the waiting vehicle, Elizabeth found herself reflecting on the journey that had brought them to this moment. From desperate resurrection workers to founders of an institution that helped children avoid such choices, the transformation seemed almost implausible when viewed in its entirety.

"You're thinking deeply," Bob observed as he helped her into the carriage.

"About paths," Elizabeth replied. "How certain choices create patterns that seem inescapable until something or someone interrupts the cycle."

The carriage began moving toward Whitechapel, where children waited who had never known Elizabeth Flanders as the Resurrection Girl or Bob Miller as a grave robber's son. To them, the couple represented possibility rather than criminality, intervention rather than exploitation.

"We can't save them all," Bob said, recognising the familiar weight of responsibility in her expression.

"No," Elizabeth agreed. "But we can offer alternatives that didn't exist for us. That's enough purpose for one lifetime."

As London flowed past the carriage windows, Elizabeth considered the strange symmetry of her life's journey. The shadows of her past remained memories of graves opened under moonlight, of Newgate's condemned cell, of desperate choices made for survival. But those shadows no longer defined her future or limited her possibilities.

The Flanders name, once whispered in connection with grave robbery and criminal enterprise, now appeared on buildings where children found safety and opportunity. The skills Elizabeth had developed through necessity, organisation, strategic thinking, and understanding of London's underworld now served constructive purposes rather than exploitation of the dead.

The carriage turned onto Commercial Road, approaching the police station where new children waited; young lives balanced on the same precarious edge Elizabeth and Bob had once navigated alone. This time, intervention would come not through chance encounter but through deliberate systems they had established precisely for such circumstances.

Elizabeth straightened her posture, preparing to meet these children with the authentic understanding that came from shared experience rather than theoretical charity. Whatever their backgrounds, whatever circumstances had driven them to Whitechapel's dangerous streets, she and Bob could offer something beyond temporary relief, a genuine alternative to the criminal paths that otherwise seemed inevitable.

The chain of criminal inheritance that began with her father's first grave robbery had finally been broken through conscious choice and dedicated service to others. Elizabeth Flanders, once known only as William's daughter and then as the Resurrection Girl, had created her own legacy, one built on redemption rather than exploitation, on creating paths forward rather than profiting from the dead.

When the carriage stopped before the police station, Elizabeth and Bob exchanged a brief glance of shared purpose before stepping down to meet their newest charges. The work continued, as it would tomorrow and the days after, one child at a time, one interrupted cycle, one alternative path created where none had existed before.